The Seaside Detective Agency

The Isle of Man Cozy Mystery Series
Book One

By
JC Williams

Home of the world's most inept private detective!

You can subscribe to J C Williams' mailing list and view all his other books at:

www.authorjcwilliams.com

ISBN-13: 978-1718680333
ISBN-10: 1718680333

Fifth printing October 2021

Cover artwork by Mikey Nugent

Proofreading, editing, formatting & interior design provided by Dave Scott and Cupboardy Wordsmithing

Contents

Chapter One
The Private Dick

Sam's dilapidated Ford Fiesta had many faults. The season dictated the level of inconvenience; in the summer, he'd overheat as the electric windows had blown a fuse, and, in winter, the heater produced less warm air than a flatulating hamster. The battery was less selective of the calendar month, losing its charge at will. Sam blew furiously into his cupped hands to warm them, but it had little effect. Worse still, the icy air in his dodgy Ford had already chilled his coffee. Whoever was in charge of the naming of things at the motor company had a poor sense of humour indeed, as *fiesta* was in fact the very last word that would have come to Sam's mind.

"Rubbish," he said, because there was little else he felt he could say under the circumstances. He cracked the door open, tossing the tepid contents of his coffee cup unceremoniously through the gap.

The outside air felt warmer than that inside Sam's car, so he held the door ajar with his foot. He took the piece of A4 paper sat on the dashboard and looked intently at the printed-out picture of a rather striking woman wearing tight Lycra running clothes. His hands trembled. He could hardly concentrate due to the throbbing pain in his frozen fingers. "Bloody chilblains," he said. He didn't actually know what chilblains were, exactly, but he'd read it in a book once and liked the sound of the

1

word. Every time his hands got cold after that, he told himself it must be a case of the chilblains.

He sat the image of the Lycra-clad woman on the steering wheel, facing him, removed his gloves, and then plunged his hands down the front of his trousers in search of some type of blessed remission and reprieve from the freezing temperatures.

"Cold, cold, cold," he said, squirming, his hands now sandwiched between the crease of his inner thighs. The moist heat produced the desired result, providing relief and warming his hands. Reckoning some friction might well enhance the effect further, he rubbed his palms against his hairy legs enthusiastically, in sharp back-and-forth motions, as if he were starting a fire. He leaned his head back, onto the headrest of his car seat, and a smile spread across his face in direct relation to the heat expanding through his digits. His eyes half-closed, he moaned in appreciation.

Sam wailed in surprise and shock as an ageing white cocker spaniel interrupted his reverie, poking its head through the door still propped open by his foot.

"Go on, you nosy little so-and-so! Piss off!" he said brusquely, his heart racing.

A petite woman with a cloud of sea-spray white hair soon appeared as well. She was slightly bent over, as if buffeted by the wind, and her weathered face exhibited enough lines as to be a cartographer's dream.

"That's no way to speak to my Terrence!" she said furiously.

"Sorry about that, luv," replied Sam. "He gave me a fright is all. I didn't expect—"

The woman stooped down, placing her head through the open doorframe. She looked at the picture propped up on the steering wheel, and then she looked at the current location of Sam's hands.

"Do I need to phone the authorities?" she asked, grimacing, the lines on her face now taking the form of deep trenches.

"What? No!" said Sam in abject horror and panic. "No, it's not—" he began. But as he yanked his hands out from their snug resting place, his watch snagged and ripped out a patch of several tender, intimately-located hairs, ripping them out in the process and causing him to cry out in pain. The pitch of his scream, unfortunately, then set Terrence to barking.

"Good boy!" prompted Sam in a desperate bid to quiet the suddenly cacophonous canine. "Who's a good doggy, then?"

Sam went to stroke the little fellow, but the cocker spaniel's furious owner whipped the handle of her dog lead around, quick as lightning, and set about lashing Sam's arm with repeated blows. She did this with such fluid, practised motions that it appeared Sam was not the first man she had bedevilled in this way.

"If you dare touch my precious dog after where those dirty hands have been, I'll slam the door on your foot and break it off!"

Sam didn't doubt her, and he tried to protest his innocence. "Look, I'm sorry. It's honestly not what it looks like. I've got a case of the chilblains, and I was worried I'd—"

"It's frightfully obvious what you were worrying!" she said sharply. "Pervert!"

She scooped Terrence up into her protective arms, sheltering him from the assailing indecency on display before them, and shielded the spaniel's eyes as if the mere sight of Sam would turn the dog to stone. "Come on, my dear baby boy, don't look at the filthy deviant."

There was no point engaging in further conversation, and, fortunately for Sam, the salty old witch didn't seem intent on phoning the police. She and her dog retreated, like the tide, from whence they came.

With that unpleasantness behind him, Sam stepped out of the car to stretch his legs which were on the verge of cramping. He'd been sat in his car since ten p.m. the previous evening and he was cold, tired, hungry, and now perhaps about to appear on an offenders' register as well. Enough was enough, he decided. It was time to go home.

"Morning," said a powerfully built man with cheeks ruddy from the chilly morning air and a moustache covered in hoarfrost. He nodded amiably at Sam as he walked by.

"Morning," replied Sam, taken by surprise once more. He was flapping his arms like a bird, at present, in a concerted effort to restore blood-flow to his extremities. Engaged in this activity, and caught unawares as he was, he'd managed to catch sight of the man's female companion only for an instant as they'd passed. Still, he knew it was her.

Sam waited for a moment for safety's sake, and then he snatched up the image. She was dressed for winter now, but her flowing auburn hair was unmistakable. He checked the picture once more for confirmation.

Sam reached into his car to retrieve his backpack, whilst keeping visual contact on the couple as they walked on, arm-in-arm, down the street.

His fingers weren't operating at levels of optimal performance, so it was taking several attempts to release the zip on his camera bag. "Come *on*," he said, looking down and furiously wrestling with the fastening, but the thing wouldn't budge. He took a breath and composed himself before giving it one final tug. "Ah. Finally," he said, as it came free.

He raised his camera up, ready now to take some shots.

"Oi, where are they?" he said, looking at the empty pavement. He slammed the Fiesta's door shut and made his way down the street towards where his targets had been, and he quickened his pace. The detached houses on the tree-lined street were opulent, only bringing the anomalous presence of his rusting car into further relief. Sam ran between the houses like a schoolboy sprinting between classrooms. *"No, no, no,"* he said to himself.

He placed his palm to his forehead, frantically looking for any sign of life. The sound of a closing metal gate drew his attention, and so he walked in that direction as inconspicuously as could a man with the onset of hypothermia (and chilblains) and a telephoto camera in hand.

A path ran parallel to the house where he'd heard the gate just closed, so he positioned himself there, readied his camera, pulled up the collar on his coat, and peered over the neat hedge that ran the perimeter of the house… but they were nowhere to be seen.

Halfway up the path, he was stood at a wooden gate festooned with a cultivated flower arch. Sam made his way to it and stood with his back to the gate (as if this should fool any casual onlooker), surreptitiously reaching for the latch, which, considering the day he'd been having, he was surprised to find open without resistance. He popped his head into the garden, but again, saw nothing.

Having no other option, he entered the garden, as casually as he could. He grimaced when he realised he still had on the woollen Mickey Mouse hat his mother had knitted him — resplendent with black woollen ears and all to complete the effect. He thought about removing it, but comfort won out as the current temperature necessitated it and there was minimal natural insulation on his balding scalp.

"Right, Sam," he said, giving himself a little pep talk. "Get in there, get the pictures, and get out. Easy-peasy-lemon-squeezy." He realized he shouldn't have added the 'lemon-squeezy' part since it only served to remind him he was in desperate need of a tinkle.

He held his camera like a sniper holding a rifle. Crouching with stealth, he progressed to the rear of the property. Fortunately, the blinds on the substantial mahogany conservatory were pulled shut. He paused for a moment — something didn't feel quite right. The couple he'd seen were relatively young, whereas the ornaments in the garden and the general feel of the house felt like it belonged to an older generation. He cautiously approached the rear window and stood on his toes to look inside. It was somewhat murky inside, as the blinds were closed, but his fears were allayed and his patience rewarded when he caught glimpse of a female form in a dressing gown walking towards the stairs.

"I know what you're doing, you cheeky girl," he said under his breath, his equipment at the ready, but she disappeared from view before he'd raised his camera.

He knew where they must be headed, and he retreated to the rear of the garden to get a better view. "And let there be light," Sam whispered in anticipation, and not a moment later, the room — what he presumed to be the rear bedroom — was illuminated in a soft glow. "Well that worked out quite well," said Sam, quite pleased with himself.

A form moved near to the window. He could make out its basic outline, but that was all. He took up his camera and adjusted the telephoto lens, zooming in to get a better view.

"Bugger," he groused, realising his view was obscured. "Curtains, open!" he said, wishing them to part, and was given a bit of a start when they did indeed open. "Yes! Result!" he exclaimed, beside himself. He had to wonder if he'd developed some sort of magic power, à la Harry Potter. "And I don't even have a wand," he said, but then realised he shouldn't have, because that only served to remind him, once again, that he really had to tinkle.

He thrust one hand deep into his trouser pocket, seeking out his 'wand', and, once found, kneading it aggressively to stave off the eruption of urine from his bladder a bit longer, just a bit longer. He hopped from foot to foot as he did this, in what might have looked very much like a happy jig to any onlooker. Fortunate for him, Sam mused, that he was the observer and not the observed.

With that minor emergency assuaged, at least for the time being, Sam took up his camera again, fiddling with the long shaft of the telephoto lens cradled in his hand in an effort to fine-tune his focus. "I've got you," he said, once sorted. "Any minute now," he added expectantly, his finger poised on the shutter-release button.

He was suddenly struck by an appalling odour, however. He assumed, for a moment, that it emanated from his armpits, but he gagged and realised that even after a night sat in his car he'd struggle to exude such as noxious smell. He looked down, scanning the immediate area for the possible source. He saw nothing that could explain it, but then a very unpleasant thought occurred to him. His lifted his leg and, sure enough, there sat several somewhat-fresh lumps of excrement underfoot — and now adhered to his shoe as well. He must have landed on it at the conclusion of his happy piss-jig.

"Blimey," he said, gagging from the smell. His diaphragm spasmed, and he fought to escape vomiting.

He tried getting rid of the mess by wiping it on the grass, looking like a horse that'd been taught to count out numbers by stamping its hoof down on the ground in quick succession — to no avail. The dog shit was nothing if not tenacious.

He looked about, searching to find something to scrape his shoe on, and caught sight of an ornate pond with an array of ceramic gnomes standing watch over it. One of the gnome guardians was proudly holding a disproportionately large shovel — which would make an ideal implement to remove the coating on the sole of his shoe. He let his camera hang down, limp, over his chest from its strap around his neck, and made his way over to the tiny pond. "That shovel may just do the trick."

The gnome sentry, for its part, said nothing. It was an inanimate object, after all, but Sam spoke to it like it was a comrade-in-arms.

"Apologies for the indignity, old son," Sam told the gnome. "It's all for the greater. Sacrifices must be made, you understand."

The gnome guardian, taciturn as it was, gave no reply.

Sam stood on one of the stone paving slabs surrounding the pool, putting his foot closer to the water. "I'll just soften the excrement up a bit in the water first," he explained to the ring of gnome sentinels. Their happy faces, moulded into grins, looked ominous in the dim light, but beyond this they betrayed no emotion. It was not their station to pass judgement one way or the other. Their job was to simply stand watch, and this is what they did.

The water level was lower than Sam first thought, so he had to lean into it further, bending one knee awkwardly, and with nothing to brace himself on for support. As his foot touched the surface of the water, Sam didn't realise it was frozen. His foot immediately gave way and his momentum spun him through the air like a circus performer. He fell arse-over-tit onto the thin layer of ice, crashing through and ending up half-submerged in the frozen water, with his head and bits of limbs protruding up through the crust of ice in the little circular fishpond like a stargazy pie.

Sam screamed in shock from the pain and cried out as the chill of the water felt like he'd been electrocuted.

"Hold it right there!" shouted a voice, dripping with the weight of authority, near to the house. And, then, "He's by the pond, Mike."

Sam tried to right himself, but the bottom of the pond must have been covered with algae and he slipped every time he tried to adjust his position.

"I said don't move!" repeated the ominous voice, much closer this time, and, soon, two uniformed police officers were stood over him. "We've got the peeper," said one into his radio. "Fancy camera gear and all. The cheek of this one."

"Peeper?" Sam chirped, as the icy water had altered his voice by way of its effect on his nether regions.

"Is that a telephoto lens or are you just happy to see us?" asked the less aggressive of the two officers with a chuckle.

Sam grabbed hold of his fortunately waterproof equipment, offering it up for inspection, and laughed along with the officer's joke. "I'm actually not a—" he began.

"I said don't move!" screamed the more aggressive of the two policemen. "You think this is funny??" He'd obviously been watching too many American films, and, convinced Sam was both uncooperative and perhaps reaching for a weapon, quickly discharged a burst of pepper spray to Sam's face.

Sam moaned in pain. "I'm not a peeper!" he cried out. "I'm a private detective!"

"A private dick, eh?" said the less hostile officer, chuckling again.

"Yes," explained Sam, using the dirty pond water to cleanse his eyes. "I've been hired to get evidence that the woman in that house is cheating on her husband."

As his vision cleared, a white cocker spaniel came into focus, trying desperately to sniff Sam's soiled shoe.

"Is this your property, madam?" asked the policeman to a startled woman who'd appeared from the house.

Sam had immediately recognised the dog, and, as if this hadn't been enough of a wreck, more flotsam appeared in the now-familiar form of a stooped-over old woman. Sam's heart sank as he realised that the woman in the dressing gown was actually the woman from earlier and not his intended target.

When she was close enough to see the spectacle in her back garden properly, she looked down in disgust. "Officer, I recognise this person. I saw this man earlier, entertaining himself in his car," she said. "He's a filthy beast!"

Sam was now so cold he couldn't muster the energy to even try and defend himself any longer.

The rather-less-sympathetic officer pulled a notepad from his pocket and flipped it open. "We had a call from a neighbour about a peeping Tom, but this, ah... gentleman, as it were... claims he's a private investigator, hired by a man to get proof his wife's been cheating on him."

"Me?" the old woman said incredulously. "I'm seventy-four years old! The chance would be a bloody fine thing!"

After a fashion, and with a phone call to his office, Sam's credentials were confirmed. With that, he shuffled to his car, soaking wet, only wearing one shoe. He had no idea which house his intended target had gone into — he was past caring — but he was getting out of there while the getting was, as they say, good.

Sam climbed into the driver's seat of his car and turned the key in the ignition... but there was nothing. The engine made a half-hearted attempt to turn over, but the sound of combustion was replaced with the all-too-familiar click-click-clicking noise and then a pathetic whimper from the engine. Sam placed his head on the steering wheel and only his frozen tear ducts prevented him from crying. The only good news was that he no longer had to pee; he must have done it already in the fishpond, either from the shock of the cold water or the fright. "I need a new car and a new job," he moaned.

$$\mathcal{P}\,\mathbf{Q}$$

Abby used her pen to twirl the errant strands of hair that ran down the side of her face, like spaghetti around a fork, and she pressed the tip of the pen to her pursed lips as she stared intently at Sam. She was jiggling in her chair like a blancmange, and trying her damnedest to stifle a laugh. It didn't appear that she'd be able to hold out much longer.

"What??" asked Sam.

Abby raised her eyebrows. "Nothing," she insisted.

"Well stop bloody staring at me, then!" said Sam.

Her barrier of self-control finally broke and her laughter, along with a tumble of words, burst forth in one continuous wave: *"On-your-arse-in-a-fishpond-covered-in-shit-oh-my-word-I-wish-I-was-there-to-see-that-HA-HA-HA-HA!"*

"It's not funny, that pepper spray hurt! Look at my eyes!" he said, sounding like a cheap hypnotist. "I'm still in pain!"

Abby was convulsing with laughter now. "Ow! Ow! Stop it, my side hurts!" she said. "You're killing me!"

Sam could see the humorous side of it all, in retrospectacle, but the skin around his eyes cracked every time he smiled. He leaned back in his chair and sighed.

"Abby, I came to work here because I genuinely wanted to be a private investigator. I knew my early as-pirations were mostly romantic notions, like uncovering a global terrorist cell or reuniting the local earl with his stolen treasure. But seriously, it's what, March? So far this year I've been a glorified debt collector, found a stolen classic car that wasn't stolen in the first place, and now I'm rolling in dog shite trying to get photographs of some randy old tart that's cheating on her husband. It's not how I imagined private investigating would be!"

Abby leaned forward, her demeanour now deadly serious. "Sam, you're not just a private investigator," she said. "You're a really *bad* private investigator."

"Abby, you're supposed to be my friend!" protested Sam. "I'm nearly jumping out of the window here!"

"You work on the ground floor, Columbo," said Abby. "If you're going to do that, at least go upstairs. Besides, it's not all that bad. At least you've got a nice car, a full head of hair, and a successful love life, yeah?"

Sam picked up a rubber squeezy stress-relief ball from his desk and lobbed it, bouncing it directly off Abby's forehead.

"Hey!" she protested.

Blimey, those stress-relief balls really do work, Sam thought to himself, as he presently felt much better.

He swivelled his chair back around and looked out the window. The view from his desk always put a smile on his face. Peel was an idyllic seaside town in the Isle of Man, steeped in history. It was a sedate experience and a complete contrast from, say, dry-humping a complete stranger on the London Tube every morning. The angle he'd positioned his desk gave him Peel Castle as a backdrop, and the beach that would be packed with tourists in the summer months. Today, however, it was pouring down and frequented only by a particularly hardy dog walker, dragging his pooch through the salty wash that sprayed over them. Or was it the other way around, the dog walker dragged along by his pooch? Sam couldn't tell from this angle.

'Eyes Peeled' was the imaginative name of the detective agency, an homage to its enviable seaside location. For an island with a minimal crime rate, many questioned the need for a PI firm at all, and, lately, Sam was starting to agree with them.

Frank, the guy in the office who nobody was quite sure what he did, interrupted Sam's daydream. "We've got a walk-in, sat in reception," said Frank, happy he had something important to say for once.

The team of investigators all looked at each other in confusion. "Are you certain?" Sam asked, searching Frank's face to see if perhaps he were taking the piss.

"See for yourself," said Frank, puffing out his chest and nodding towards the reception area. He looked very pleased with himself. No one ever turned to him for answers.

Sam craned his neck, but he didn't have a good view of the reception area from where he was sat. "I can't…"

"We've never had a walk-in," Abby interjected. "Four years and not one person has walked in off the street."

"They have today," replied Frank, shuffling paper in an attempt to look both industrious and important.

"Maybe they've come into the wrong office by mistake?" offered Sam. "What do they want?"

Frank looked down his nose, over his glasses, studying the lined notepaper on his clipboard for several long, arduous seconds, tracing his finger from one line to the next. There were no actual notes written there, but no one else could see that, and all eyes were turned to him. "Hmm. Not sure," he replied, finally.

"Why did you just look at your…?" asked Sam, shaking his head. "You know what, never mind. Look, she's probably lost her cat or something. Can you get some details from her, Frank, and I'll call her back later on?"

"She's hot," said Frank, and you could tell he'd been waiting for just the right moment to drop the other shoe.

"ON IT," replied Sam immediately, taking a tie from his drawer. "I've got this one."

Sam walked down the corridor to the virtually redundant interview suite, adjusting his tie as he went. The blinds were partly open, and Frank hadn't been wrong — the woman looked stunning, from what he could see. He opened the door with vigour, adopting the persona of a professional, sophisticated PI.

"Sam Levy, at your service," he said, in an artificially deep voice, closing the vertical blinds for dramatic effect.

Sam took a seat directly opposite where she stood, her back to him. She was admiring through the window the view of the Peel Castle, it seemed. Sam was also admiring the view from where he sat. She wore an elegant 50's style floral swing dress and straw hat, which brought an element of colour to an otherwise overcast day. She added to the air of mystery by continuing to stare out of the window.

Sam cleared his throat. "How can I help?" he asked.

"You're a private investigator?" she replied.

"I am. How may I be of service to you?"

She turned and sat across from Sam, who was now taken aback by a glorious smell of perfume and her classic beauty which was enhanced only by her immaculately applied makeup.

Sam was as vacant as a feline after catnip. She took her hat off and shook her auburn hair, which brought him back to his senses like a slap in the face. He leaned back in his chair as the realisation hit him: *That's the bloody woman I was following.*

He shifted in his seat uneasily, unsure what were her motives.

"I'm being followed," she said softly but firmly. "I've been to the police, but nothing has been done. It's been going on for weeks."

"I don't mean to offend, Missus...? Miss...?" Sam said, clearly poaching.

"I'm not married, and my name is Beth," she replied.

"Beth. What makes you think you're being followed, Beth?" continued Sam after an awkward silence.

"I've seen several people following me. I just know. Someone was following me just yesterday, and he wasn't the first."

Sam started to sweat. "And, em, where was this?" he asked.

"Near to the house I'm staying at, but this one looked scruffy, like a vagrant. Also, he smelt awful when I walked past him."

"He was probably in his stakeout clothes, which he'd usually leave in his car, hence, the smell?" offered Sam, weakly.

"What?" she said, cocking her head slightly.

Sam swerved it. "That is, do you know why anyone should want to follow you?" he asked, regaining his deep-voiced yes-I'm-a-professional-PI affectation.

She stared at him with her intense brown eyes. "People have their reasons," she said cryptically. "You don't need to concern yourself with the why. I just want you to find out who it is that's following me. If I know who that is, I can figure out the rest."

Sam eventually returned from the meeting with his tie half undone and impressive sweat patches under his arms.

"She must have been nice," said Abby in reference to the dark, damp patches on his shirt. "Are you okay?" she asked when there was no response.

Sam struggled on his answer. "I'm not sure. I've just been given a job that I'm pretty sure even I can't muck up."

"Oh, and that would be?" asked Abby.

"I've just been hired to find myself," he said.

"You mean spiritually?" Frank asked, expecting a laugh. He was met only with stern looks, however, as his moment was now clearly over. He looked down at his desk and shuffled some papers, pretending to busy himself.

Sam elaborated on the meeting, checking through the notes he'd taken.

"Sam," said Abby in an assured tone, once he was done. "Sam, surely you have to tell her there is a conflict of interest?"

"Of course. I will. But, technically, due to me being useless, I didn't technically find her — I just happened to be in the vicinity. Plus, she didn't recognise me."

"You need to tell her!"

"I will," Sam insisted. "But there's something going on here. She said she's being followed by several persons, plural. So it's not just me. She also said she wasn't married!"

"So she lied. So what?" asked Abby.

"Well someone's lying, but that doesn't mean it's her. She is very pretty, after all," Sam explained.

"What does her being pretty have to do with whether she's lying or not??" said an exasperated Abby.

"Whoever hired us to follow her insisted she was his wife. That's clearly a lie," Sam replied, ignoring Abby's objection.

Abby now stood over him. "How are you going to tell her you've completed an investigation and managed to find yourself? She'll think you're mental and probably phone the police, and the last thing you need is any further police scrutiny."

"Yes," Sam agreed. "But the thing is, she's clearly nervous and unsure who's following her. I know I'm *one* of them, but if there are several others who've also been following her, who were *they?* And more importantly, why were *they* following her?"

"So, how do you see this one panning out?" asked Abby.

"Well, the person who's paying me must also be paying the others, I imagine," Sam mused.

"But *he's* your client, not *her!"* Abby protested.

"Yes, Abby, but he's lying by saying she was his wife," Sam explained patiently. "And what do we actually know about this guy? The job came in over the phone, and we've never met him, see? So I'm actually *helping* her by taking her money to look for myself. At least this way I can figure out what exactly is going on, and, importantly, for her, who else has been following her." And, then, "She *needs* me, Abby."

Sam was proud of himself. He strutted back to his desk like a resplendent peacock.

"This is all going to end in tears," declared Abby.

Sam tapped his pen on his desk. "There's something going on here. I don't know what it is, but it's big. I've got a feeling about this, I tell you, and when Sam Levy has a feeling, he…"

But Sam had lost his intended audience as Abby, bored, had got up and left the room. Undeterred, Sam took the picture of the woman he had out from his desk drawer and sat back in his chair, gazing at it, and stroking his chin thoughtfully.

"You're hiding something, Beth," he said aloud to no one but himself. "And Sam Levy is going to find out what that is."

Chapter Two
The Little Explorer

There was something captivating for an inquisitive child visiting the Isle of Man, with glens to explore, hills to climb, and countless beaches to forage for discarded treasure. As a boy, Sam couldn't understand his friends who'd want to sit on a plane for hours to sit, in the end, bored, next to a swimming pool, dripping with sweat. In the weeks leading up to his summer holidays, Sam would pester his grandparents who lived on the isle with thoughts on where they should visit — often to previous locations where he hadn't completed his exploration. Six weeks, two with his own parents to keep them company, simply wasn't enough. His grandparent's house was a quaint fisherman's cottage with a view over the Port St Mary harbour that was absolutely breathtaking. A narrow road separated the cottage from a stone-covered beach, where he'd look for washed-up exotic-coloured glass polished over the years by the salt in the sea. Sam would always complain that he couldn't go on the beach when the tide was in.

He'd never forget the summer of 1984, sat on the seawall as the waves lapped below, where his feet dangled.

"I've made this for you, Sam," his grandad had said with a broad smile. "It's a coracle — a small wooden boat for you to paddle around the harbour when the tide's in."

It was, and still remains, the greatest gift that anybody had ever given him. Sam could recall the mien of pride on his grandmother's face, looking on from their white wooden porch as her husband handed over what he'd been working on the entire year between summers.

At the end of the school holidays, he was pleased to catch the ferry home and see his parents, but the feeling of leaving the island, and his grandparents, was awful. He'd count the days till he could return once again.

In later life, Sam lived all over England, but wherever he worked he'd always ensure he was no more than a few miles from the sea. He'd been happy on his own, but then he found Lilly, the love of his life. She was intelligent, beautiful, and ambitious. Sam didn't want to live in London, but he followed his heart and settled down — in a cramped, one-bed flat near to Canary Wharf where the monthly rent was the price of Sam's first car.

He was devastated when his grandparents both died within a few months of each other, but they knew that by leaving the house to their 'little explorer' the house they loved would be cherished. Sadly, Lilly didn't settle into the more placid way of island life and wanted to return to London. This left Sam with a difficult choice: what colour he'd decorate after she left.

The dark, bitter-cold days of March gave way as the optimistic flower buds in Sam's garden indicated spring had finally arrived. Sam stood — as he did every morning — in the doorframe of the compact wooden porch outside his stone cottage, drinking his morning cup of tea.

The track outside his gate was a popular route for tourists to circumnavigate the pretty seaside town. There were several cottages in a row — all oozing a nostalgic, nautical theme — and those passing couldn't resist peering over the ornate garden wall to absorb the feeling of a time gone by. Sam was the perfect host and would frequently invite inquisitive passers-by in for a drink of something. It was part of the charm, and the reason he enjoyed waking up there.

Sam smiled as a young child scampered over the seawall, followed closely by his parents struggling to keep up. It was something he'd done numerous times himself as a child — and many times since, returning from the pub at the conveniently located Albert Hotel.

"Morning!" he called out, raising his cup up in salute before draining the contents.

It'd been at least two weeks since he'd last heard from Beth, and he was starting to think that there wasn't anything to uncover after all. If anything, he began to think she was a bit of a crackpot. She wouldn't give him her phone number, for starters. Nothing new there, for Sam. But, from a client, that was unusual. She would insist on phoning in for any possible updates from him, but, unfortunately, despite his best efforts, there was nothing to report. He'd stopped following her, so there was that. So at least she had one less person showing an interest and pursuing her.

$$\mathcal{P}\,\mathbb{Q}$$

"What time do you call this?" asked Abby, before he'd even had a chance to take his coat off.

Sam scowled back. "And good morning to you, also!"

"I told you I had something to show you!" she said, foraging through her oversized handbag for her notebook.

"I know," said Sam. "But I assumed it was going to be, well, boring. Anyway, it's still before nine a.m. so I'm not exactly late. Where is everyone?" he asked in reference to the office looking like the deck of the *Mary Celeste*.

"Cheeky bugger! I do so tell you interesting things!" replied Abby. "And the rest of them have been called into

Harry's office. It looks as if the office of five is soon to become two."

"What??" exclaimed Sam, with clear panic in his voice. "Is he laying people off?" He cradled his face in his hands. "I need this job. Nobody else would ever employ me."

Abby shook her head. "Don't worry, Harry called over the weekend to let me know. He said he'd tried to call you. We're the only ones who actually do anything, it would seem. And, being honest, knowing how little the two of us have done lately, it really shows you how much the others have been doing. Or haven't been doing, rather."

"Bloody hell, Abby, I don't think I realised how much I like my job until I thought I was about to lose it. I'm really going to step up my game and bring new business in the door. I'm going to take this more seriously and be more professional."

Abby rolled her eyes. "Sam, you do realise that you've got two different shoes on? Anyway, look what I found out," she said, typing on her keyboard. She sat back and pointed at the screen.

Sam looked decidedly underwhelmed. "It's an article about the most powerful women in the art world?"

"Yes!" said Abby, waiting for the penny to drop. "And…"

"And what?" said Sam, staring blankly at the screen.

"Look at number four on the list," said Abby. "God, do I need to spoon-feed this to you?"

Sam's eyes widened. "That's Beth!" He read the contents of the article. "She's worth over a hundred million quid?? Doesn't that take the biscuit! I should really have tried harder with her!"

"Are you missing something?" prompted Abby. "Anything?"

Sam screwed his eyes up, on the pretence of thinking really, really hard.

"Anything at all?" prompted Abby a second time.

Sam screwed his eyes up a little harder. He was afraid if he screwed them up any more, he'd pull a muscle.

"Sam," said Abby flatly. "What's her name?"

"Beth," replied Sam, giving her a look. "I may be an idiot. But I'm not a *blithering* idiot. Give me *some* credit, Abby."

Abby nodded towards the computer, pointing at it with her whole head.

"Oh! Wait there a moment," Sam said, finger at the screen. "That's Beth, but they're calling her Emma Hopkins. Why are they calling her Emma Hopkins? Bloody hell, so she lied to me?"

"Exactly! I'm surprised to admit this," said Abby. "But your gut feeling that there was something further to this whole thing? It may actually be correct."

"But, what use is the information to us?" asked Sam. "Beth, or whoever she is, has buggered off. So there isn't any particular reason for us to get involved anymore. We could chase her up for her outstanding invoice, but I didn't really do anything to warrant getting paid. Anyway, how did you find out about this?"

"I'd like to say it was using my brilliant powers of deduction, but, in reality, the bloke who employed you to follow her called up this morning..." Abby replied, pausing at the end for dramatic effect.

"And?" asked Sam impatiently.

"I told him to sod off, told him that we knew he wasn't her husband."

"Did he admit it?" asked Sam.

"He did, and it was him that directed me to this website. He said his name is Mr Justus, but I'd be surprised if it really was. But he also admitted the real reason why he wanted us to find her..." said Abby, making sure to pause yet again for dramatic effect.

"Stop doing that!" said Sam. "It's not an episode of Poirot, and nobody's watching!"

"Well, apparently..."

Dramatic pause.

"Out with it already!" said Sam, replicating his happy piss-jig by dancing in place excitedly.

"The mysterious Beth. Or Emma," Abby continued, to Sam's great relief. "Is currently in possession of a painting that was stolen from him. A very, very expensive painting. He had word that she'd be on the island, at some point, which is why he employed us."

"The plot thickens," said Sam, doing that stroking of the chin thing again. "But if he's already lied to us once, how do we know he's not talking rubbish again?"

"I asked that," said Abby. "And I wasn't quite as polite as that, either." She tapped the keyboard again, bringing up onscreen a further article detailing the theft of the painting.

"The painting's worth four million quid??" said Sam, reading the article. "Gordon Bennett!"

"It is. You can understand why our chap was so eager to get it back."

"So why doesn't he just go to the police, then?" asked Sam.

"Good point, and I asked him that very same question. He says he wasn't interested in arrests — he just wants to get his painting back."

"Sounds a bit dodgy, all this," said Sam. "We should just tell him we're not interested."

"Sam!" shouted Abby. "You're the one who keeps telling me you want to get involved in something other than chasing up outstanding parking tickets! This is your chance, our chance, to get involved in a proper investigation. Plus, he's giving us twenty-five thousand pounds up front, and another seventy-five if we reunite him with his picture."

"I think I need to sit down," said Sam, the colour draining from his face. "That… that would pay the wages around here for a fair bit, I should think."

"Exactly! If we don't do this, it'll be a few weeks before we're taken into the old man's office as well, only to be told the office is closing down. This could be the only chance we have to save the business."

"What sort of name is Mr Justice, though?" said Sam, musing. "Not the cleverest of false names."

"No, not Justice. Justus," Abby said, correcting him.

"But that's what I just said," Sam protested.

"No. Justus. As in, not everyone else. Just–us."

As if on cue, Frank walked through the office, looking forlorn.

"Hey, Frank, I'm sorry to hear you're leaving us," said Abby, trying, not entirely successfully, to sound sincere.

Frank packed the contents of his desk into a small cardboard box. "I can't believe that he's letting me go," he said dismally. He looked over at Sam. "And he's keeping a halfwit like you? You haven't even got matching shoes on."

"Don't let the door hit you in the arse on the way out, Frank," Sam answered.

Abby moved in for a closer look at Sam's footwear once Frank was gone.

"You've seriously got to do something about your shoes, Sam. They're not even the same colour."

Sam shrugged his shoulders. "Abby, when you're this good-looking, the last thing people are going to notice are your shoes. Besides, we've got work to do — we're looking for an art thief!"

Chapter Three
The Irish Sea

I'm sure it was your turn to buy lunch?" said Sam, placing a tray on the wobbly metal table.

"Don't you just love eating al fresco?" said Abby, avoiding the question.

"It's only a plate of sausage and chips, Abby. You really are a cheap date."

"I know, but look at that view!" said Abby. "And what's wrong with sausage and chips? I love sausage and chips!"

The sun glistened on an Irish Sea as calm as a millpond. Contented tourists enjoyed the walk along the promenade clutching an ice cream as they'd done for generations. Abby smiled as she spied a toddler on the beach strike the base of a bucket and squeal with delight when the bucket pulled free, revealing a perfectly formed sandcastle.

"Don't you just love it when the sun shines?" she said enthusiastically.

"The sun always shines," Sam replied. "We don't always see it, is all."

Abby was a couple of years younger than Sam, and, unlike him, was born on the island. She'd worked in finance and qualified as an accountant. It took her exactly two years to realise that sort of life was not for her. She'd tried every career path that would keep her out of an office, including running a nursery, of both children's and the flower variety, a vet's assistant, and even a blackjack dealer.

She had an expressive, cheery face, which held a noticeably healthy glow for someone who rarely wore makeup.

"Oh. Are you wearing dungarees?" asked Sam, when quite plainly she obviously was. "I didn't realise they were something that people still wore?"

For most women, denim dungarees with a white t-shirt would look too casual, but Abby looked interesting, especially with her brown curly hair tied in bunches.

Abby looked slightly offended as Sam backtracked. "No, sorry, I wasn't being rude. I think it looks good. It's a good look. You look nice. It looks... nice." His face turned crimson.

"Are you alright?" asked Abby. "You suddenly look ill."

"No, it's just, em... the vapours," Sam sputtered, scrambling for an explanation.

"The vapours?" Abby replied, not believing what she was hearing.

"It happens sometimes," Sam answered, committed to the lie now, despite having no actual idea what in fact the vapours even were.

"Maybe you should pay your GP a visit about it?" Abby suggested, her eyes twinkling with mirth.

"It'll pass. It always does," Sam assured her.

"You are a very strange man," Abby opined, though not unkindly.

A rude seagull with minimal table manners broke the brief silence that followed by swooping down and taking a sausage off Sam's plate. Sam jumped back in his chair. "Little bugger!" he shouted, as the bird struggled to get airborne with its meal clutched firmly in its beak. Sam's arms flailed as he tried to defend the rest of his meal. "The beaky blighter has got my lunch!" he shouted, to the amusement of two elderly women walking next to the outdoor cafe.

Amidst the ensuing battle of wits between man and bird — in which Sam was clearly outmatched — the precariously balanced table was tipped over, sending its contents spewing over the paved terrace. The bird took its leave and flapped furiously as it tilted up its beak defiantly and gulped down the sausage in one go like a gannet.

Sam reached for his remaining sausage before it rolled under Abby's seat. In one fluid movement, he launched it in frustration at the bird. "Have another, then, you thieving little devil!" he called after it, releasing the sausage like a javelin thrower.

The porcine-based projectile flew perfectly, though missing the bird by inches, and unfortunately continued its trajectory towards the old women that had been chuckling at Sam's misfortune. Sam watched in horror as his lunch headed with the speed of a Tomahawk missile, homing in on the back of their heads. It came to an abrupt halt as it landed in the bluish hair of the fragile-looking woman on the right. Her gentle perm welcomed the sausage like a hair clip. "Bloody birds coming after me!" she said, shuffling forward, and in reference to the jarring sensation on her head.

Sam hopped on the spot, unsure whether to retrieve his lunch, but on balance decided it was perhaps better time to settle the bill and take his leave.

"You can't leave her like that!" cried Abby.

"She'll be fine," insisted Sam.

"Sam, she's got tomato sauce running down the back of her coat."

"Ah, it's okay, you can't even see it. Maybe it fell out...?" Sam replied. "Oh, okay, fine, I'll go and get it," he then said, relenting.

Before he'd moved an inch, however, the elderly pair were set upon by a flock of gulls looking for an easy meal. "It's nineteen sixty-three all over again!" one of them shrieked, and, for ladies of a certain age, they certainly knew how to run when it mattered.

"Well, that was interesting," said Sam.

"Things certainly took a *tern* for the worse," Abby offered.

"I'm still hungry," Sam answered, the joke flying right over his head. "Come on, I'll buy you an ice cream instead."

With that accomplished, Sam licked his mint choc chip with one cautious eye looking out for flying invaders. Then he took a notepad out of his pocket, which surprised Abby as he'd never used one before.

"I've been making a few enquiries with contacts in the art world," he said. "The thing that's been bugging me is why Emma Hopkins is over on the island in the first place."

"Maybe she's got family here?" suggested Abby, using her tongue to prevent a drip down her cone.

"I thought that," said Sam. "But the bloke who employed us didn't know why she was going to be here."

Abby shook her head. "No, he just knew she might be here, but didn't say why."

Sam took a torn-out newspaper fragment from his trouser pocket. "Seemingly, this Emma Hopkins is a serious player in the art industry. She's got galleries in Milan, New York, and London. And as well as selling art, she's apparently an accomplished artist herself. The interesting thing is that her experience extends beyond painting. She's also a collector and seller of ancient artefacts."

"Ooh, like Indiana Jones?" asked Abby.

"Exactly! Take a look at this," said Sam, thrusting the newspaper cutting towards her.

She read for a moment. "That simply cannot be a co-incidence, can it?"

Sam smiled. "An art thief on the island at the same time as one of the most important Viking artefacts comes up for sale. It does seem a little strange."

"The auction is tomorrow!" exclaimed Abby, getting more animated and waving her ice cream like a wand. She continued to read. "The auction estimate is one-point-two million pounds for the Viking cross. Cripes, Sam, she must be here to steal it!"

"Has to be," said Sam smugly. "Abby, we're going to our first art auction!"

"It's not my first," said Abby.

"What?" asked Sam.

Abby looked slightly apologetic. "I know you said, *Abby, we're going to our first art auction*, for maximum impact, but, I thought I should mention it, you know, and that I've already been to one."

"I'm not going to lie, Abby, you have taken the tarnish from my moment, and I'm not sure it's that important," said Sam, with a half-smile.

"It is, because my Nana took me with my mum, and we..."

... The ice creams melted long before Abby came to the end of her not-entirely-relevant anecdote about her first visit to an auction. Sam wasn't overly interested in who bought or sold what, but he was enjoying this; he was enjoying working, as part of a team. He enjoyed working with Abby.

🔍🔍

For a small island, the heritage on display — including the Manx Museum — was enviable, proudly showcasing the isle's ten-thousand-year history. Since she was a small child, Abby relished a visit to the museum. There was something enchanting about the experience — the smell, the lighting, the feeling you were looking through a porthole into a different time.

The Art Gallery was a fascinating visual insight of Manx history spanning hundreds of years. Resplendent oil paintings of the ancient Lords of Man kept company with pencil drawings created by prisoners housed on the isle during WWII. Today it was host to a high-profile auction of antiquities and art that had caught the attention of collectors the world over.

The substantial room was teeming with row-upon-row of plush red velour seats with gold trim. A stage stood at the head of the room with a wiry-looking auctioneer with mad-professor hair making last-minute preparations behind his lectern — gavel in hand, ready for the day's action.

"Sorry, that's taken," said Abby, again, looking anxiously at her watch. The room had filled quickly, and keeping the reserved seat open was proving a challenge. She checked her phone, once again, to make sure it was silent, but also to see if Sam had been in contact.

"Where the hell *is* he?" she muttered under her breath. And, then, "Sorry, that seat's taken," she said aloud to a disappointed lady.

The auctioneer brought matters to order and there was a hushed silence as the crowd listened intently to the introductions. Abby was pleased with her position — discreetly at the rear — which gave her visibility over the audience. Key to the operation was her ability to remain unseen. And being inconspicuous was certainly the order of the day here.

At the opposite end of inconspicuous, the imposing entrance doors opened with a cringe-worthy screech as the ageing hinges protested the weight like an arthritic knee. It was akin to fingers down a blackboard, resulting in a large number of people turning in frustration. Shoe heels then proceeded to clomp heavily as they made their way across the highly-polished wooden floor, interrupting the solemn occasion and causing even more people to turn their heads.

Abby didn't even need to look. She just knew.

"Abby?" said a voice whispered, though projected well enough that all could hear.

She buried her head in her coat.

"Abby?" the voice persisted.

At this point, the auctioneer was about to throw his gavel at Sam.

"Ahem! If there should be present an Abby, would you be so kind as to raise your hand and let yourself be known so that this, em... gentleman, as it were... could locate you?" he announced, with no attempt to hide the annoyance and disdain in his voice.

Abby reluctantly raised her hand, allowing Sam to find and take his seat — only after those already seated had to slide their chairs back on the polished floor, creating even more noise.

"Sorry, oops, sorry, excuse me," he whispered, waving discreetly at Abby as he made his way over to her. "Sorry I'm late," he said through the side of his mouth once sat beside her. "Good seats," he remarked. "At least no one will see us."

"Shhh!" said a shrill voice from behind.

Abby eventually removed her head from her coat and looked Sam up and down.

"What the hell are you wearing?" she said through her teeth.

Sam brushed his hand with his jacket. "A tuxedo," he said proudly. "You told me to dress smart."

"Sam," she said, exasperated. "I meant only to not wear a t-shirt, and make sure you were wearing matching shoes for a change."

"I look smart, though?" said Sam, fishing for a compliment.

Abby was starting to lose her composure. "Sam, you're wearing a bloody tuxedo!"

"I know. I hired it this morning."

"Sam, you're wearing a tuxedo at midday and we're trying to remain inconspicuous."

"Shhh," was repeated several more times.

Abby and Sam sat enthralled, once the affair began, as the auctioneer ran effortlessly through the catalogue — and the sums bid were staggering. Four assistants stood at the side of the room, juggling several phones and monitoring the action on their website. The novelty soon wore off for our intrepid pair, however, and Abby and Sam began to guess how much the next lot would go for.

"Three-hundred thousand pounds," said Abby, in reference to an aged landscape painting that was being paraded at the front of the stage. "Definitely no more than that!"

"No chance," said Sam. "That's got to be at least five-hundred thousand."

The bids increased, and they soon surpassed £300k... £400k... £500k...

"Yes!" said Sam triumphantly, punching the air in celebration.

"And we now have five-hundred-and-fifty-thousand pounds," said the auctioneer, pointing directly at Sam.

"Did he just point at me?" asked Sam, with panic in his voice.

"Yes," said Abby. "Don't move a bloody muscle, and you better start praying that someone wants that painting more than you. Either that or get ready to run!"

Sam scoured the room, willing someone to raise their hand. The man with which he'd inadvertently entered a bidding war was poised, caressing his greying handle-bar moustache as if he hadn't a care in the world.

"Going once..." said the auctioneer, pointing at Sam once again.

"Put your hand up, you pompous-looking old twit," said Sam between clenched teeth and a tortured smile. "Please, please put your hand up."

"Going twice..."

Abby moved to distance herself. She wanted nothing to do with this.

The gavel was about to strike the sound block and Sam could feel the carotid artery in his neck constrict.

"Six-hundred-thousand pounds!" announced the auctioneer, pointing his gavel at the other bidder who looked, perhaps, like a retired colonel.

"Yes!" said Sam in relief.

"Is that six-fifty?" the auctioneer asked Sam.

Sam waved his hands furiously. "No, no!" he said. "Don't take any more bids from me!" he insisted, clutching his chest.

The auctioneer scowled at Sam's coarse language.

"For our first undercover operation, this isn't going quite to plan," Abby confided. "We would be less conspicuous if we'd arrived riding a pink unicorn with fireworks flying out its arse."

"Shhh!"

"Oh, *shhh,* yourself," replied Abby, picking her bag up. "Come on, Sam, let's get out of here."

Sam placed his hand on her arm. "Hold up," he said. "Over there. Front row, black dress. That has to be Emma Hopkins?"

"It is!" said Abby, craning her neck, and clutching his arm in return. "Right, it must be happening today. What-ever happens, don't let her out of your sight — I can't see her very well from this seat because of that pillar in the way."

"Do we phone the police?" asked Sam.

"We should," said Abby. "But we'll never find the stolen painting. Plus, she's not actually done anything yet."

"The next item has attracted considerable interest," announced the auctioneer. "A fabulous example of a ninth-century Viking cross. Where shall we start? Three hundred thousand?"

It was a popular item, judging by the flurry of bids and animated waving of arms by those clutching phones.

"It's good, this," said Sam. "I need to buy a metal detector and find one of those Viking crosses to sell."

"You make sure you keep your hands by your side and keep an eye on the front row," said Abby. "And you do look quite smart. Totally inappropriate. But smart."

Sam smiled. "Thanks," he replied as the auctioneer smashed his gavel down. "Oh. I missed it," said Sam. "How much did it go for?"

"One-point-six-million pounds!" Abby replied.

"Cheese and crackers!" exclaimed Sam.

"Aw, did you want to buy it?" she teased.

"No, there's now an empty seat on the front row and Emma has gone."

"One bloody job you had, Sam!" said Abby. "Where the hell is she? Surely she's not going to be as brazen as to rob the thing in broad daylight??"

Sam jumped to his feet and marched — noisily — to the front of the room looking completely out of place in his current attire. If not for his earlier interruption, people on the first few rows would have likely assumed he was handing out canapés.

"There's no need for alarm," he said, addressing those in attendance. He turned his right hand above his head, as if he were taking off a top hat. "Sam Levy, Private

Investigator, at your service." He'd clearly been watching too many low-budget detective films.

"Get off my stage, you buffoon!" shouted the auctioneer, ready to hit him with the gavel for the second time in one afternoon.

Sam pointed to the cross. "My partner and I are here to prevent a very serious crime. We have credible information that the cross in that glass cabinet is the target of a robbery planned for this day!"

There was an audible intake of breath, which, being honest, Sam was hoping for.

"Preposterous!" said the auctioneer. "By whom?"

Sam was getting into his stride and took a couple of causal paces up and down the front row for dramatic effect. "By the woman who was sat in the front row who has now mysteriously disappeared!"

"That's because I'm stood over here," said a startled female voice. "As I've just been to the loo."

"Ah! Well! Ah! Okay, then," said Sam, struggling with his words. "This is, em… this is an interesting development indeed," he added, attempting to keep hold of what little dignity yet remained. He lowered his right hand just in time to watch Abby skulking toward the exit at the rear of the room. Sam thought about running too, but the auctioneer was stood in front of him, snarling.

It couldn't get much worse as Sam took a step back. "We… or I, as it would now appear," he said, attempting to explain himself. "Have it on good authority that the woman over there, as it were, Emma Hopkins, was primed to steal the artefact in question on this very afternoon."

"Steal it, you ignoramus? She's not trying to steal it!" shouted the auctioneer, taking a step closer to Sam — who was faltering by the second.

Sam's voice was now breaking. "How... how, do you know that?"

"How do I know?" the auctioneer repeated like a sanctimonious parrot. *"How do I know?* I know she wasn't going to steal it because she's the one who's bloody selling it!"

The blood drained from Sam's face as a cold sweat ran down his back. He stammered, but he was like a boxer swaying after receiving a volley of uppercuts.

One man in attendance had apparently seen enough. Smartly dressed in a navy suit with an open-necked shirt, the unidentified man picked up his brown leather briefcase and walked discreetly for the exit, taking his phone from his inside pocket as he did so. Once outside and believing himself to be out of view, he stood outside the museum entrance and lit a cigarette as the phone dialled out.

"It's me," he said in a gruff voice. He listened for a moment, taking a drag. "Yes, it's her," he said. "Yes, I'm sure."

He took a couple steps forward before speaking again. "I understand, Mr Justus," he said, blowing the contents of his lungs skyward. "I'll get it back, yes. And the only way she'll be leaving this island is in a box."

Chapter Four
Staying Alive

This is a new low, even for me," said Sam, stomping along Douglas Promenade on the way to Abby's car. "I've been thrown out of most places. But a bloody museum? That's got to be a first."

Abby was failing to stifle her laughter. "I'm sorry for leaving, but it was just so awkward I couldn't watch any longer."

"It wasn't exactly a walk in the park for me, either! They all started laughing at me when they realised I wasn't some sort of cabaret act. One woman on the front row thought I was a magician at one point."

Abby bit her bottom lip. "Where's your bowtie?"

"He's got it. The bloody auctioneer. He grabbed hold of it and tried to use it like a dog lead to drag me out. I had the last laugh because it was on elastic and snapped in his face. Anyway, now who was the guy with the cigarette you mentioned?"

Abby grabbed her phone. "I stood outside waiting for you when a guy walked out shortly after. I got this photo of him, but it's not the clearest. He was on the phone and I overheard him say someone — a woman — was going to be going home in a box. And not only that, but..."

Dramatic pause.

"Out with it, woman!"

"Before he hung up..." she continued, after sufficient time as to ensure Sam was fit to burst. "... he called the person..."

Sam could feel the lower half of his body twitching. It was near to starting another piss-dance.

"... Mr Justus."

Sam stopped dead in his tracks. "Holy hand grenade, they have to be talking about Emma Hopkins."

"Correct," said Abby. "It would seem that Mr Justus is not only employing us but this chap as well," she added, pointing at the image captured on her phone. "But the only difference is, we're not trying to get her *killed*. We need to let her know!"

Sam scowled. "The last person she wants to see is me, especially as I've just stood in front of a packed room accusing her of something she didn't do."

"She will..." Abby said.

Dramatic pause.

"... If she wants to stay alive."

"You know, that was good," said Sam. "I do have to admit."

"What was?"

"That *if she wants to stay alive* bit. You've really got this down to an art, Abby. All that was missing was the *dern-da-dern-dern deeeern* tune to finish it off."

"Thanks!" Abby grinned. "And how did Emma take it, by the way? The whole accusation thing, I mean."

"Oh, yes, she was delighted. Thrilled, in fact. She was especially receptive when I emptied the contents of her bag on the floor looking for something incriminating?"

"Looking for what, a crowbar, or a black bag with *SWAG* written on the side?" said Abby, sarcastically.

"I don't know. I panicked because I could see the security guards running towards me and it was the only thing I could think of doing."

"How far away have you parked?" asked Sam. He looked like he'd stayed out all night and was on his way home doing the 'walk of shame' with a stinking hangover, since, as a result of being wrestled to the floor by several security guards and assaulted by the auctioneer, Sam was looking rather dishevelled with his jacket pocket ripped and scuffed suit trousers.

"We're close now," Abby told him.

"You're right, Abby, by the way," said Sam. "We need to tell Emma that her life is in danger."

Abby nodded. "That guy looked pretty mean. Like a Mafia stereotype."

"But he hasn't reckoned on Sam Levy, has he?" Sam swelled his chest up like the tide. "You'll be okay, Abby, I'll look out for you," he added, throwing his jacket casually over his shoulder. He didn't have a firm enough grip on the collar, however, and it slipped from his fingers, with the jacket falling to the promenade floor and landing flat into a puddle of salty sea water.

Abby distanced herself as Sam retrieved his jacket, flapping it in the wind to shake the water off. "You know, if you shake it more than a few times..." she began.

"What?" Sam asked, distracted and otherwise engaged.

"Nothing," Abby replied. "I just feel so much safer, is all, knowing you've got my back, Sam," she added.

Sam couldn't take offence, not with the look of genuine mirth on Abby's face and her eyes twinkling like moonlight reflecting off ocean waves.

"So. That Emma. She's pretty cute, I think you're in with a chance there!"

"She is indeed," replied Sam, with a faraway look, before snapping back to his senses. "What? Oh. Emma? Ha!

Not hardly, I should think. Ruined my chances there, I'm afraid."

"One never knows," Abby replied with her playful selkie grin.

"I've got more chance of getting my deposit back on this suit rental," Sam groaned, flicking sand off the jacket sleeve.

$$\wp\,Q$$

Sam sat with his shoes off, resting his feet on the corner of his desk. Abby could always tell when he was thinking because he'd rub his bald head like it was a comfort blanket.

He tapped his pen on his desk. "You know what I don't understand, Abby?"

"Nuclear fusion? Speaking Tongan? Why birds suddenly appear, every time you are near? I could go on," laughed Abby.

"Besides those things," Sam replied, throwing her a look. "Emma is obviously not short of cash and owns galleries all over the world. She sold a Viking relic for over a million yesterday. So why would she be involved in the theft of a painting? It just doesn't make any sense."

"I can think of four million reasons," said Abby.

"I know what you mean, but, why would you risk your reputation, career, and possibly your life for a painting? Which is expensive, granted. But if she's already rich, what real difference is that going to make? We're missing something here, Abby, but I can't place my finger on what it is."

"I'll tell you what I do know," said Abby. "The old man will go mental if he knows we're spending our time on this with virtually no chance of making any income from it." She took a compact mirror from her bag, puckered her lips, and applied a layer of pink lipstick.

Sam had his back to her. "Are you squirting perfume over there?" he asked, sniffing the air.

"Yep, I've got a dinner date tonight," she replied.

Sam nearly dislocated his shoulder the speed he spun around on his chair. "I didn't think you were seeing anybody?" he said as casually as he could muster. "You're not getting back with Pete, are you? He was such a knob."

"I know he was a dickhead, which is why I split up with him," Abby replied. "I'm just going to dinner with a friend. Nothing serious. It's just nice to go out for something to eat."

Sam squirmed. "I'd, eh, you know, if you were bored one night, take you out for something nice. Not chips, either. Something special. You know. Served on a plate."

"On a plate?" Abby chuckled. "Well, then."

He screwed up his face. "Served on a plate," he repeated flatly, then sighed miserably. "What the hell does that even mean? Abby, you can understand why I'm single when I talk to you like that. What hope have I got in the real world?"

Abby gave him a sympathetic smile. "You'll find someone special." She patted his head. "After all, how many men in the Isle of Man can honestly say that they're a private investigator? The women will be like putty in your hands," she said. "Don't work too late!"

Sam wondered why women would be like pudding in his hands. Sometimes he didn't understand Abby's jokes.

The smell of Abby's perfume hung in the air long after she'd left. Sam sat at his desk looking over to Peel Beach and the families making the most of remaining sunlight. He felt a bit down, somewhat deflated. He was finally working on a case of substance, but he struggled with a nagging self-doubt. He'd always convinced himself that, given a proper assignment, he'd pull out all the stops. Work never usually got him down, so why was it doing so now? He laughed as he recalled the state of Abby's face as she skulked out of the museum, looking mortified as he slowly died in front of everyone.

"Sweet cheese and crackers!" he said in a moment of realisation. "Am I in love with Abby?"

Sam couldn't think straight; he thought it was work, but maybe it wasn't? When Abby told him she had a date, he felt like he'd been kicked in the stomach. He needed solitude, he needed time to think. He picked up his newspaper and headed for the one place where he could collect his thoughts, free from distraction.

He tried to read the paper but nothing was sinking in, so he just sat, staring at the door. It was quiet. He was the only one left in the office, so he panicked when he heard a vague noise from the reception area.

"Hello!" he shouted. "Abby, is that you?"

There was no response, but the noise immediately stopped. His heart raced.

"Abby," he said once again, but nervously this time. "Very funny. Did your date let you down?" he managed, his voice quavering despite his attempting to sound self-assured.

There was no response, but Sam could hear the muffled sound of footsteps.

They were getting nearer.

"Come out with your hands up!" boomed an American voice, without preamble.

Sam shat himself, which was fortunate considering his current location. He made a noise in response, but it wasn't coherent — more of a pained wailing noise derived from his sense of abject fear.

"I won't ask you a second time!" shouted the voice. "If you don't come out now, right now, I'm busting down this door!"

Sam heard what sounded like a gun being cocked. His mind raced: *It must be that Mafia-looking guy Abby saw.*

"Last chance!" said the ever-more-impatient voice.

"Okay, okay!" Sam squeaked. "But I'm not…"

"I don't care! Open the door! Now!"

He didn't have a phone to call for help, and the only way out was the door he had no choice but to now reluctantly open. Sam shuffled towards the door, trousers and underpants around his ankles, and took a deep breath.

"I'm unarmed," he pleaded, holding his arms smartly aloft once he'd opened the door and released his hand from the knob.

Two men stood before him, recoiled in disgust, as Sam presented himself to them.

"Good god, man, you could have pulled your pants up!" insisted one of the men.

Sam stood with his arms still above his head. "But I–I couldn't," he stammered. "You told me to open the door straight away. And… and I've not wiped yet."

The two men could see that he wasn't a threat, and they allowed him to return to the toilet to sort himself out.

"You're American?" asked Sam tentatively after re-emerging, the paperwork on this last job of his having been satisfactorily completed. "Are you working for Mr Justus, then?"

The two men were dressed immaculately in dark suits with black overcoats, which, in a seaside town made them standout. Sam breathed a little easier when the gun held in one of the men's hand disappeared from view, retracting back behind his coat.

"Do me a favour?" said the chiseled-looking man on the right.

"Yes?" said Sam cautiously.

"Can you close the bathroom door? It's not a good smell."

"Of course, sorry." Sam complied with the request. The last thing he wanted was to anger these fellows and see that gun drawn back out.

"You know this woman?" asked the man on the left, thrusting a printout in Sam's face.

He stared for a moment, unsure whether to plead ignorant, but not knowing who they were and the fact they were armed, he reasoned this wasn't the best option.

"I might," he offered. "But, believe me, I'm starting to wish I didn't. That's Emma Hopkins?"

"Well, that's *one* of her names. I'm Agent Tanner and this is Agent Weiss. FBI," said the fellow with the chiselled face authoritatively, as if this should explain everything.

Sam started to laugh. "Shut the front door!" he said.

The two agents looked at each other in confusion. This wasn't the typical reaction to which they were accustomed.

"We're being serious," one said.

"Very serious," said the other.

"Shut the front door!" said Sam once again. "You think I'm that daft? Who sent you couple of halfwits, anyway? Did Abby put you up to this? Or what about cock-eyed John in the pub? Was it him? It was him, wasn't it?"

The two men looked at each, temporarily at a loss as to how to proceed.

"Do you lot honestly expect me to believe that the FBI have sent two agents all the way over to our tiny little island?" said Sam, his confidence regained.

"Now you listen—" one of the men began.

Sam stupidly went on the offensive. "Where did you get your guns? Toys R Us? Let's have a look," he said, reaching towards the closest man's coat.

This was precisely and incontrovertibly the wrong thing to do. Before he'd touched fabric, Sam felt like he'd been attacked by a revolving door. He lay face down with his nose pressed into the cream floor tiles, with so many parts of his body in pain he couldn't isolate the different bits. He was a sea of pain in a world of hurt.

"We are agents of the FBI," repeated one of the agents, his knee pressed firmly against Sam's spine, in a manner which suggested that there were no two ways about it. "This is not a joke, and I urge you to take this very seriously for the sake of your own welfare. Are we clear?"

"Y–yes," Sam managed through shallow breaths, as, at present, he could not breathe especially well.

They allowed Sam to lift his head by two inches — just high enough to inspect their badges.

"Sir, I'm going to let you up now, but do not reach for our guns again. Ever."

They helped Sam to his feet.

"Sorry about that, guys." Sam gasped, trying to refill his lungs with air. "I thought… I thought it was a wind-up. We don't exactly get many FBI agents in these parts, as you can well imagine."

"What's your relationship with this woman, and where can we find her?" asked one of the agents less than sympathetically, all business.

"Can I sit down?" Sam asked. "My legs are a little bit wobbly."

After taking a seat, he continued, "Look, I don't know where this woman is, and, as for my relationship, there isn't one. As you will have deduced from the sign outside, I'm a private investigator."

"You're a PI?" one of them interjected. "Seriously? I thought you were the receptionist or something."

"I thought you were the cleaning guy," said the other.

"I'm a private investigator," insisted Sam, offended. "Do I look like a—?"

"So who are you working for?" interrupted one of the agents.

Sam shrugged. "I'm actually a bit in the dark on that one myself."

The agents were getting impatient and annoyed. "Well, who's paying your bill?"

"Ah," said Sam. "Don't tell my boss, but I don't think there is a bill to settle. See, originally, we were employed to find her. And when we did... well, when we did, we were then employed by *her* to find out who'd employed us to *find* her. Do you follow me?"

"Not—" one agent began.

"Yes, we follow you," said the agent with the face chiselled from granite. "Who employed you to follow her and why? And you mentioned a Mr Justice. Who is this Mr Justice? Is that some kind of codename?"

Sam was about to correct the agent but then, with self-preservation foremost in his mind, thought better of it. "That's the name we were given," he simply said. "We were originally employed by this person — who we've never met — to find that woman," he explained, pointing to the picture in the agent's hand. "We were told that she was cheating on her husband and asked to get proof. Presumably, for the divorce hearing. That woman eventually told us there were several people following her, and she tried to hire us to find out who."

"Yes, yes, we get that," said Agent Tanner. "Will you get to the point!" His fingers were twitching because they weren't wrapped around his gun at the moment, and that made him very anxious.

"Okay, okay," replied Sam, rather offended that he was being rushed along and not allowed to tell his story at his own pace. "Right. So. Mr Justus told us — over the phone — that the reason he wanted to find her was because she'd stolen a painting from him."

"Interesting," commented Agent Tanner, his stone face betraying no emotion. "And where is she now?"

"How would I know?" Sam said, shrugging.

"You're a private investigator?" Agent Weiss suggested.

"So, why would the FBI be involved in the theft of a painting?" asked Sam. "She must have done something else? Something more nefarious?"

"That information is on a need-to-know basis only," said Agent Weiss.

"And you don't need to know," added Agent Tanner. "But you can be assured that we haven't travelled thousands of miles to appreciate the sunset," he said, with a wave of his hand, in reference to the warm glow behind Peel Castle.

These fellows did have a flair for the dramatic, Sam thought to himself. He'd certainly give them that. And he only wished Abby were present as she would surely appreciate it.

"We need to speak with her," said Agent Weiss. "If you see her, you need to phone us right away," he added, handing Sam a business card.

Sam looked in awe at the embossed business card. "So... technically, I'm on a special assignment with the FBI?" he said. "Sam Levy is working with the FBI?"

Agent Tanner stepped forward and thrust a meaty finger in Sam's face. "If you tell anybody we're here, you'll be visiting Davy Jones' locker. Don't forget to phone us if you know where she is."

"I need to tell my partner Abby," insisted Sam.

"You're telling nobody!" came the response.

"But I'll have to," Sam explained. "I work with her every day. She'll be onto me in seconds if I don't."

The two agents huddled for a moment. Agent Weiss emerged. "Okay. Just her. And tell her that this remains *strictly between us.*"

"Can I also tell my mum? You know, about me working for the FBI?" Sam asked, emboldened by the concession.

The hard look on Agent Tanner' face, now at the door, told Sam everything he needed to know. Once they were gone, he turned the key in the latch. He fell back on the door and took several deep breaths.

"Sweet Baby Jesus," he said, staring at the business card. "Sam Levy is working with the FBI." A giddy smile crept across his face. "Abby's going to be impressed with this!"

Chapter Five
The Del Monte Man

The arrival of an Embraer Phenom 100 jet at Ronaldsway Airport went pretty much unnoticed on an island so involved in the finance sector. It eased gracefully into the executive jet centre, where an immaculate black BMW sat with its engine idling.

When the ground crew gave the signal, a short, stout man with slicked-back receding black hair appeared on the top step, giving a cautionary glance. He took his aviator sunglasses from his jacket pocket before taking one final look around.

He nodded to his colleague — who was still on board — and they made their way to the foot of the stairs like they were forming a guard of honour. First to deplane would be a slim brunette, dressed simply but smartly in denim jeans and a fitted white t-shirt. She was, however, not rising from her seat. She squinted as the sunlight reflected through the windows, lighting up her face. For someone travelling in such an opulent manner, she didn't appear to be too appreciative.

Eventually, the woman had no choice but to make her way to the exit. The two men both extended an arm to help her down, but she didn't proceed, rather, shifting furtively, as if looking for some other option.

"Come, my dear," said a voice behind her. "Mr Swan, are we ready to leave?"

She had nowhere to manoeuvre, reluctantly taking the hands offered to her as she walked down the steps and then towards the open door of the waiting BMW.

Her polite escort smiled. "So. This is the Isle of Wight?"

"Isle of Man, Mr Esposito," replied his corpulent assistant, cautious about offering the correction.

"Whatever it may be called, I do not intend to be here longer than necessary."

His white linen suit was remarkably wrinkle-free considering the long flight. As he joined them in the car, he replaced his cream fedora hat, completing an ensemble which, one might assume, must have been loosely inspired by the Del Monte man.

"I like this," said Mr Esposito, as the car sped from the airport. "I always love the countryside. And what about you, Marilyn?"

"It's Madeline," the woman said in frustration. "I've told you that three times. Why did you have to bring me with you?"

"And I have told you, my dear," he repeated in a thick Italian-American accent. "You are my insurance policy. If I have you with me, then your little sister will not be inclined to do anything, shall we say, foolish."

She shifted impatiently on the plush leather seat. "Honestly, I'd rather you'd cut my fingers off and posted them to her. Like any self-respecting kidnapper would have done. At least, then, I wouldn't have had to put up with you lot for the last two days."

"Trust me, beautiful," said Mr Swan, sat next to her. "If your sister doesn't play ball, it won't be your fingers I'll be cutting off."

Madeline groaned like a child who'd been told to clean their room. "Please, can you start with my ears? Then at least I won't have to listen to you any longer, you odious cretin."

Mr Esposito laughed. "I think she is quite fond of you, Mr Swan. Tell me, Mr Swan," he continued. "Has our man on the ground made contact with Ms Hopkins, or is she still remaining... elusive?"

"No sign, Mr Esposito. The sale of the Viking cross went through, and we've got people monitoring the airport and the ferry terminal. We know she's on the island, and there's no way she's going to get off it without our knowledge."

"Very good," said Mr Esposito. "We can then enjoy the charms of this enchanting island until we meet up with her. And the sale of the cross went as expected?"

"One-point-six million pounds, Mr Esposito."

"Excellent news, Mr Swan. Can we double our efforts to find Ms Hopkins? It would be a shame if we were to have come all this way with her sister and not be able to arrange a family reunion. Madeline, you would be appreciative of a family reunion, would you not?" asked Mr Esposito, getting her name right this time, and pronouncing the last syllable of it with the long vowel sound, like 'brine'.

Madeline tried to free her arm, which was being gripped tightly. "Drop dead, asshole!" she said with venom.

"Say the word, Mr Esposito, and I'll I throw her out the car."

Mr Esposito raised his hand. "No need, Mr Swan, but thank you. You see, Madeline, Mr Swan is what I would consider to be a loyal employee, someone I would trust with my life and often have. If my employees are good with me, then I am exceptionally good with them. Would you agree, Mr Swan?"

"I agree, Mr Esposito. Exceptionally good."

"Good god," said Madeline. "I think I just threw up a little in my mouth. Why don't you two get a room?"

"No need, Mr Swan, thank you," Mr Esposito said, raising his hand once more. "Madeline, I do not take betrayal too kindly. One of my problems, and I do have them, is that people see the cheerful face..." He motioned towards his face with a flourish of his hand. "...polite speech, and friendly disposition, and they mistake this for weakness. Do you think I am a weak person, Madeline, someone who is easily taken advantage of?"

She was brave but she wasn't stupid, choosing, this time, to remain silent.

"Good," said Mr Esposito. "If you thought I was weak, that would have made me very sad. What I find particularly upsetting is when employees betray me. You can imagine how distressed I was when I heard that you and your lovely sister — who I see as partners, mind you, rather than employees — had developed, unexpectedly, a moral compass and had attempted to betray me. You can understand why I would find such a thing especially disappointing, can you not, Madeline?"

Again, she thought discretion was the better part of valour and kept her mouth shut.

The car came to a halt at a level crossing, allowing a steam train to cross the road in front of them. Madeline gave the door handle a furtive glance and considered her chances at making a bolt for it. The grip on her arm had been relaxed, and the occupants of the car captivated by the steam engine. She felt a mixture of amusement and disbelief at the sight of three armed, hardened criminals waving gleefully at the passengers on the train like they were out for nothing more than a pleasant Sunday drive.

They were about to pull away, once the train had passed, and she knew this was the best chance she'd have at escape, but she also knew it was useless. She had no phone, money, purse, or even a passport.

Mr Esposito must have sensed her unease. "Relax, my dear. Your pretty eyes have a frown, and you do not want to get wrinkles. We will soon be on our way home, do not worry. We simply need to have a little chat with your sister. See if we can talk a bit of sense into her. This is all. *D'accordo?*"

$$\mathcal{P}\,\mathcal{Q}$$

Sam was in to work early. Very early. He hadn't been able to sleep, and his second coffee of the morning had done little apart from prompting a bowel movement. His knuckles pushed into his cheekbones, supporting his head as he looked vacantly at the energetic joggers taking advantage of the empty promenade. He'd spent the remainder of the previous evening mulling over whether to update Abby or not about his meeting with the FBI. Ordinarily, he would have thought nothing about texting her at stupid o'clock, but this had been different. This time she had been on a date, and likely preoccupied with... well, preoccupied — he didn't want to think about with what. There were notions he could entertain, of course. But he didn't want to even let them in, much less entertain them.

"Morning!" announced Abby cheerily as she entered the office, and she said it with an unusual (and disheartening, as far as Sam was concerned) amount of gusto. "You're in work early, are you not?" she asked, and continued on before he'd even had a chance to respond. She said like a whirlwind dancing across the waves, "I think this office is too big for us now, what do you think, do you reckon the old man will look to move us elsewhere, to a smaller office, Ooh, I don't think I want to move from here, I mean, look at that beautiful view, I do love that view, I don't think I'd want to give that up, I've always loved—"

"Have you taken something?" Sam interrupted, in reference to the speed at which she was speaking.

"What?" asked Abby, hanging up her jacket. "Taken? No, why do you ask?"

Sam shrugged his shoulders in an attempt to appear disinterested. "You just seem... wired, is all."

"Oh, are you on your second coffee already?" she asked, swirling around in the pot Sam had made what little remained, and without waiting for his answer. "Today, young Samuel, I am in a really fine mood. The sun is shining, the gulls are calling, and we're working on an interesting case!"

"Which may not pay us," said Sam, his words like a cold fog.

"Which may not pay us, correct, but is, at least, interesting!" Abby chimed in, undaunted.

She had her hair in bunches. She always looked cute with her hair that way, Sam thought wistfully. He tried to act as nonchalantly as possible. "Did you have a nice evening?" he asked.

Her face lit up. "Wonderful!" she beamed. "We went to that new little Italian. The food was fantastic, you really must go!"

Sam collapsed deeper into his chair. "Oh, yes, I forgot you were on a date last night," he said, lying. He was desperate to find out who she was with, of course, though without saying it outright. "Did he... em... dress nice?" he asked, somewhat less-than-cleverly.

"What? Did he dress nice? Since when were you the fashion police? You're just fishing to see who I was with!"

"Pardon?" said Sam casually (if unconvincingly so). "Sorry, I wasn't listening, and I wasn't fishing!" he protested.

"See, you *were* listening!"

"I just don't want to see you making stupid mistakes again," said Sam, more to the truth (if leaving out one important consideration most pertinent to him). "Your choice in men has historically been, let's just say... questionable."

Abby screwed up her left eye. "They've not all been awful!" she said.

Sam spun round on his chair in one fluid motion whilst using his fingers to count on. "Your last three boyfriends have been complete tossers! The first of them — was it Ritchie? — that Neanderthal forgot your thirtieth birthday. And the second—"

"All men forget things," Abby said, stopping him short.

"Not all," said Sam, countering. "For instance, you're not my girlfriend and yet I still know that your favourite film is Chitty Chitty Bang Bang — no judgement here — you love Belinda Carlisle songs, oh, and you love Dirty Dancing. The film, that is, not the action. Although you may like that also?"

"Aw, Sam that's sweet. From anyone else, I'd be thinking about a restraining order. But that's lovely," Abby replied with a smile. "Maybe it's the two of *us* that should be going out together," she added with a laugh.

Sam looked to the floor, worried he was so transparent that Abby could see right into his thoughts.

"Anyway, Sam," Abby assured him. "You needn't be worrying about me, because my wonderful dinner date last night was actually with a lady friend, Emily, who shares my love of cheesy films!"

Sam came to attention in his chair, his ears perking up and his mood instantly improved. "You're not... you know... experimenting with Emily, are you?"

"What, no, of course not, she's an old friend visiting the island," answered Abby. "Wait, hang on, what do you mean by *experimenting*?"

"Well, you know..." he said. "Kissing... and things. Like that."

Abby threw her head back and laughed.

"Because..." Sam continued on. "It's just that, if you *were* in fact experimenting, I would expect you, as a friend, to tell me every single detail, okay?"

Abby did not immediately respond, so Sam took the opportunity to fill the silence. "Details are important," he said. "Especially in our business."

By this time, she had formulated a response. "Rest assured, you will be the very first to know about such a situation," she told him. "I'll notify you straight away, how's that? In fact, I'll phone you *during*, if you like?"

"I can see we're on the same page here," added Sam merrily, nodding his head in earnest agreement.

Sam was indeed pleased, not about the offer of a phone call, but that she hadn't had a date. He didn't know what to do with this information, exactly. But he took a selfish pleasure in knowing she was single, and that his concerns had been nothing more than a storm in a teacup. He had regained his confidence.

"I had a visitor last night," said Sam without any introduction. "Well, two of them, as it happens. I was going to ring you, but I didn't want to disturb you. I had a visit from none other than the FBI."

"Shut the front door!" replied Abby.

Sam nodded. "Yes. That's exactly what I said. On more than one occasion."

Abby had already lost interest and had picked up her phone to make a call. Sam pressed the receiver back on its cradle. "I'm being serious," he told her, and he gave her a look that he hoped would convey that seriousness and get the point across.

It seemed to do the trick, and, now he'd got her attention, dropped the business card onto her desk. "These two came to see me," he said, tapping the card. "And trust me, they saw more of me than they wanted! Anyway, I checked their credentials on the FBI website after they left and they're legitimate."

Abby scrutinised the business card. "What the hell do the FBI want with you?" she said after a moment ruminating.

"They didn't want me. They wanted our friend, Emma Hopkins," he told her.

"For what?" Abby asked.

"They wouldn't say. Couldn't say," replied Sam. "Only that they wanted to speak to her."

Abby twisted her hair thoughtfully. "What about Mr Justus?"

Sam shook his head. "No, I mentioned his name, and, unless they're great actors, I don't think they knew who he is."

"Interesting," said Abby, drawing out the word into separate syllables. "So we've got an art thief on the island being followed closely by an associate of the alleged victim, Mr Justus, and to make matters even more interesting, the FBI has shown up. This would make a bloody good book," she remarked, chewing on a tuft of hair. "The problem that's been mentioned before is, we don't know who to believe. We don't know who we're working for, and, most importantly, we don't know who to send an invoice to!"

"Are you saying we walk away?" asked Sam.

"Hell no," said Abby. "I need to know what's going on. The worst-case scenario is that we keep the twenty-five thousand Mr Justus sent us. That'll keep us going for a while. If he's on the level, and we get the painting back, we get another seventy-five. If he's not on the level, I'm sure some insurance company will be interested in the return of the picture."

"Fair enough," said Sam. "But, where does that leave us? What's next for us?" he added before realising what he'd said, and how it might sound.

"Hmm?" said Abby.

"For the case, I mean. What's next for the case?" he said, burying his head in the computer screen, his cheeks hot.

"Emma Hopkins. Or Beth. Whatever she calls herself. Is the key to this. So we need to find her," said Abby. "She has to be staying somewhere, and there are only so many hotels on the island, and it's a small island. We need to exhaust all of our resources and do some right proper investigating."

"She's not going to have the stolen painting with her, though, surely. And it's not like we can lock her up," said Sam. "And if we find her, who takes priority? Mr Justus or the FBI?"

"Who's paying us?" said Abby.

Sam thought for a moment. "Good point! Okay, how about we concentrate on finding Emma Hopkins. If and when we do find her, if there is no sign of the painting, which I suspect there won't be, we hand over her location to Mr Justus."

"But what about that lunatic I saw outside the museum, who said she was going to be going home in a box? It's probably not the best idea to send some crazed hitman in her direction," Abby offered.

Sam rolled his eyes. "Abby, this isn't *CSI Miami*. It's some bloke looking for his picture. How about we tell Mr Justus at the same time as the FBI? That way we're doing what we were paid to do, and, we don't face the wrath of the law. Plus, the FBI will make sure Emma Hopkins doesn't end up at the bottom of the Irish Sea wearing concrete galoshes."

"Okay, Sam," Abby agreed, nodding her head. "That sounds like a plan." And, giving a sharp clap like a sports coach would do after a pep talk and the team returning to the pitch, "Let's get this show on the road!"

Sam took several deep breaths as he looked down, bracing himself against his desk. "Abby, this may sound a bit weird," he said, finally, pushing himself upright. "Abby, I'm not sure how else to say this, but I wondered if possibly... I could take you out for a drink? Possibly something to eat? Nothing cheap, I'm talking a nice meal, steak or lobster... or both. You know, if you wanted."

There was no answer.

"I could even catch the lobster," he said, fumbling now, and he gave a nervous laugh. "Abby, I'd really like it if I could take you out on a date."

There was still no response, and he was filled with dread, thinking he'd overstepped the mark. He spun about, but she was gone. He heard the beep of a horn, and there she was, waving enthusiastically from the front seat of her car. She gave him another quick toot for extra effect.

Sam lifted his right hand and waved to her through the office window, with only the tips of his fingers. "I'd catch a lobster," he said softly.

"For you, I'd catch a lobster myself."

Chapter Six
Catching the Ferry

The third and final boarding call for the 08:00 sailing to Heysham echoed through the substantial waiting room, packed with those on the first leg of their holiday and also returning tourists who sported a more dejected demeanour. The Irish Sea could often be cruel, but the favourable weather ensured a pleasant crossing would be the order of the day.

A polite queue formed, which snaked from the entrance door to scanners where security staff worked furiously to process the passengers. Far from the crowd, in the darkest recess of the hall, stood a man and a woman, giving the appearance of two lovers preparing for an emotional separation. She pressed her back to the considerable glass windows which gave a view of the commercial containers being driven onto the ship. In spite of the considerable heel on her shoes, she had to stand on tiptoe to look longingly into her male companion's eyes. Her hair was hidden by a cream headscarf which revealed the slightest wisp of a black fringe. Her eyes were obscured by oversized tortoise-shell sunglasses, which completed a styling that Audrey Hepburn carried so well.

It would be apparent to a keen observer, however, that, as she darted her head furtively, her attention was not on her lover but rather the crowd of people behind him. She arched her neck and scoured every inch of the room.

"Henry, I think we're good to go," she whispered to her companion.

After a final glance, satisfied, she let her heels drop back down to the floor, adjusted the collar of her coat to conceal her face, and eased out from her position of seclusion.

Her companion grasped her arm suddenly. "Emma, stop!" he warned her in a quiet but urgent voice, as an overweight man in a cheap, ill-fitting suit approached them, a look of solemn intent over his face. His gut, most unfortunately, flowed over his belt and the bottom button on his shirt, its battle with the man's prodigious girth lost, was splayed open allowing the unwelcome view of a hairy stomach.

As the intruder drew near, Henry curled his hands into tight fists.

The man reached into a leather briefcase as Emma instinctively stepped back. *Not here. Not with all these people*, she thought.

The fat man's skin was clammy, and sweat ran down his face, as his outsized hands rummaged clumsily through his briefcase before finally revealing a green clipboard with A4 paper attached.

"I'm from the tourist board. Time to complete a visitor satisfaction survey?" the porcine man said, breathing hard.

Henry turned his head and smiled. His muscles uncoiled slightly, but he was still prepared for any untoward action that might yet present itself.

"Piss off, tubby," Henry said. "Before I stick that clipboard up your arse." Henry was built like a rugby player and spoke like he was from good stock, and dressed to encourage that perception in his tweed jacket and matching tie.

The man — Derek, according to the now visible badge on his lapel — took the insult in stride. He was accustomed to abuse, it seemed. "If there was any aspect you didn't enjoy, I'd be happy to help?" he offered, unaffected.

"I'm not enjoying *you* just now," Henry told him. "So how about you eff right off, fat stuff."

Derek soon took the hint — he was, again, fairly accustomed to abuse — and retreated like a wounded stag. Or like a harpooned manatee, as the case may be. "Portly people have feelings, too," he mumbled sadly to himself as he took his leave, his shoulders drooped in despair.

"Come on," said Henry, ushering Emma as he took the window of opportunity. They linked arms and joined the rear of the diminishing queue, whilst remaining vigilant.

"I don't like this, Emma. It's too open," Henry said through his teeth.

Emma lowered her head and used her hand to cover her mouth. "We don't have any other option, Henry," she said in frustration. "They've got the airport covered, and, apart from this ferry, the only other course of action available in getting off this rock would be to bloody well swim."

The security scanners were agonisingly close as Henry reached into his pocket for their boarding cards. "Bleedin' hell," he said desperately. "Over there, by the toilets. Two men with their backs to us."

"So?" asked Emma.

Henry narrowed his eyes. "The man on the right is using his phone in selfie-mode to covertly observe who's in the queue."

"Henry, he might just be taking a picture?" she suggested, more in hope, before continuing, "Henry, this is our last—"

"Let's go," interrupted Henry, as the two men took to their feet. As the two men approached with purpose, the shorter of the two, on the left, raised the flap of his jacket to reveal what looked very much like a cattle prod, tucked into the waist of his trousers.

Henry raised his hand. "Derek," he said, before repeating slightly louder, calling after their recent acquaintance. "Derek! About before. My apologies. You caught us at an awkward time. My colleagues, over there," he said pointing towards the two men. "They had some comments about their stay they were anxious to convey. I suggested they speak with you, my fine fellow."

Derek's shoulders lifted up, and, his spirits now buoyed, said, "Ah! Very kind of you, sir. And, rest assured, I'll feedback anything they've got to say." Derek sailed in the direction of the two men, tacking left and right, expertly navigating around wayward passengers towards his destination.

The two would-be assailants were soon to be intercepted and held at bay, at least for the time being.

"We can still make it onto the ferry," said Emma. "The gate is still open."

Henry headed towards the exit shaking his head, pulling her along by her hand. "No, if they're here, there could easily be others aboard the ferry."

"But what choice have we got?" Emma protested.

"If we catch that ferry, we're stuck for four hours with nowhere to escape. We need to stay here and come up with another plan, Emma. It's the only way."

"Well you go, then!" Emma put forward. "You've got nothing to do with this mess and they're not after you."

"I'm going nowhere," replied Henry. "If they kill you, who else is going to employ me?"

Meanwhile, with a fluid grace that belied his bulk, Derek approached his two eager new clients whilst retrieving his green clipboard. He applied the sincerest of smiles to his face that he could muster — which wasn't difficult, as he was convinced the two men were in desperate need of his services. "Excuse me, gentlemen!" Derek cooed. "I understand you've got some feedback you'd like to convey about your visit to our lovely isle?"

The two men looked through him like he wasn't there (which shouldn't have been easy, given his girth), but Derek was nothing if not persistent. He stood directly in their path, and he clung to them like barnacles on the hull of a ship — nothing could prise him off.

The two men were effectively rendered dead in the water, at least for the time being (and providing a welcome distraction for Henry and Emma to distance themselves).

"All feedback welcome!" Derek chirped in a polished, well-rehearsed fashion.

In response, the shorter, stout man brushed his jacket aside and drew the prod from his jacket like a Wild West gunslinger. Before Derek even had a chance to unsheathe his pen and lick the tip, he was lying on the floor, convulsing.

All in all, Derek wasn't having a particularly good day.

"There's your feedback, my old son," said the assailant, closing his jacket once again. "The service is... shocking."

The two men made their way around Derek's prone figure, giving him a wide berth. Once clear of the obstruction, they looked about, but by now their intended targets were nowhere to be seen. They stood outside the terminal building, alone, and, now they'd time to reflect, the taller of the two men shook his head in disappointment.

"That is the first time you've had a chance to use your new toy," he said.

"Yes," the other replied, patting the bulge under his jacket happily.

"And that is seriously the best line you could come up with?" the first man asked. "I have to say, it's a bit, well… underwhelming."

The second man now looked forlorn, the wind taken from his sails. "I know, but the pressure got to me," he said. "I was hoping to use *'bolt-out-of-the-blue'*, but it didn't feel like the right circumstance. I'm upset with myself, if I'm being honest. I've let myself down."

"Hello, Mr Esposito," said the taller man, phone to his ear. "Yes, sir, they were here." He listened for a moment before continuing. "No we couldn't get them, there were too many people. Too many witnesses. But the good news is that they're still on the island and we'll find them soon. We were about to get them when, unfortunately, we had a… well, a bolt-out-of-the-blue."

The two men walked towards their car, parked opposite the terminal building. "That was my bloody line," said the shorter man, now disconsolate.

"Aw, don't blow a fuse," said the taller man.

"Dammit, that one is even better," admitted the other, climbing into the car. "I should have used that one. I might go back in and electrocute him again, just so I can use that line," he said. "Oh. Too late," he added in reference to the ambulance, blue lights flashing, approaching at speed to attend to Derek. Who never did manage to fill his daily quota.

Chapter Seven
Call Me Lloyd

Abby drew her car up against the kerb. "This is definitely the street?" she asked again. "You're sure?"

"Of course I'm bloody sure. You tend to remember the places where you've nearly been arrested," Sam replied, pointing very cautiously to the house where the elderly woman lived with her dog, as if he were afraid the mere act of pointing might alert the leather-faced old woman to his presence. "That's the house I *thought* they went into. So I can say, for certainty, that we should avoid that one. Because it turned out I was wrong."

Sam was staring at the house, unable to turn away, as one might do with a terrible car crash on the side of the road, so did not see Abby shake with silent giggles. She spared him any cutting remarks, unwilling to put salt in his wound as he suddenly looked very vulnerable.

"In fact, am I even allowed to be on this street?" Sam wondered aloud.

"Did you get a restraining order against you?" asked Abby, a question she didn't expect to be posing.

"No," replied Sam in a frightened whisper.

"Well then, you're fine," Abby assured him. "Just don't go near the old woman's house this time."

"No danger of that," Sam replied, flinching as something akin to a pee shiver ran through him.

"Nice houses!" Abby said cheerily, looking up and down the street. "I could definitely see me living in this neighbourhood."

Sam's thoughts drifted off into a more pleasant direction, as he imagined carrying Abby on their wedding day over the threshold of their opulent, newly-purchased house.

"Sam! Are you with me?" asked Abby.

"Yes, definitely," Sam answered dreamily. "Hang on, what? Yes, who? What were we...?" he continued, after snapping out of his reverie. "Ah. Of course. I'm right here with you. Ready for action. At your service!"

"What did I say, then?" asked Abby in reply, in the sort of tone all mothers and most schoolteachers had perfected to an art.

Sam lowered his head. "I, em... I wasn't listening. Sorry," he said, timidly.

Abby issued forth an exaggerated sigh before carrying on. "Which way was Emma Hopkins heading?" she asked in the exasperated manner one might speak to a slow-witted child that was nevertheless well-loved. "When you saw them walking down the street."

Sam pointed, indicating the general direction he'd seen Emma Hopkins going. "But just make sure we don't go near *that* house, just there. That's the old sea witch's house," he added.

"Oh, there's no *we* here. You're staying in the car," informed Abby. "We need to find out where they'd been staying, and the last thing we need is to be arrested in the process."

"That's fine," said Sam, pulling something from his jacket pocket.

Abby's attention was elsewhere as she tried to figure out which house she should approach first. She tapped her fingers on the steering wheel in quick succession, with the chorus of light thumps sounding like rain on the roof. "I think I'll knock on that door," she said, finally. "I'll make out like I'm due to meet my new work colleague, but I've forgotten which house they're in. I'll describe Emma, and, hopefully, someone must know where they were."

Abby looked to Sam for approval, and she nearly smashed her head off the driver's side window as she did a double-take.

"What on earth are you wearing??" she asked, half in shock and half with uncontrollable laughter. "Oh, my god, where's my camera!"

Sam's lower lip drooped, along with his pride. "I thought it'd help me. You know. With surveillance, and all that."

"A bloody wig! What ever possessed you to go and buy a wig? Oh, I can't get out of the car now," said Abby, who by now had a flood of tears running down her face. "I can't breathe," she said, snot bubbling at the bottom of her nose. "My stomach," she said gasping. "You bastard, I'm in pain, I can't look at you."

This continued for the next few minutes. It was like the first time you wear your glasses in public; you're not sure if you'll get a compliment, or, in this case, for Sam, the absolute and complete guts ripped out of you.

"My jaw hurts. Oh, my jaw hurts..." continued Abby, wiping tears from her cheek and still in uncontrollable spasms of mirth. "What the hell? It doesn't even fit! And the fringe, you look like Lloyd from *Dumb and Dumber*... *AH-HA-HA!*" she screamed. "That's it, I'm going to call you Lloyd from now on!"

Several more minutes, once again, passed by for Sam, as Abby now had her head buried into the steering wheel, with her shoulders heaving.

"Look," said Sam, by way of explanation. "When you've not, you know, got a lot of grass on the pitch, a baldish head can stand out in a crowd. That's not very good if you're trying to be discreet. As we are now."

"Trust me," said Abby, the tears at last subsiding. "You're not looking discreet wearing that. If you're seen in public wearing that, you'll end up on some sort of register. I'm not entirely sure which. In fact, they may have to start a new one just for you!"

It was impossible for Sam to get angry at Abby, and so he accepted the constructive feedback — or sustained assault — and moved to remove the offending article. "It was quite nice, at least, having a covering on top once again if only for a bit," Sam confided. But, then... "Cheese and crackers, it won't budge."

"You'll sort it out," Abby assured him. "I need to go and knock on a few doors. Stay in the car, and try to keep out of sight."

Sam bobbed his head up and down as he continued to struggle in his efforts to remove the wig — which Abby took to mean a nodding of agreement. She chuckled as she stepped out and closed the door behind her, shaking her head in dismay. "Lloyd," she said to herself. "Amazing. Honestly, you'll be the death of me yet, Sam Levy."

Sam folded down the sun visor and took what he imagined to be one final look at the wig. "It's not that bloody awful," he said. "Not entirely, anyway."

He pulled at the wig once again, trying his darnedest to tug it off, but it didn't budge. He wondered if he was gripping it correctly? He looked in the mirror, once again, and repeated the process. "Damn," he said, as his head jerked each time he yanked, but the wig refused to come off.

He took a firm hold and braced his neck as he yanked it once again, but there was no give. He was now in a pitched battle with his own head — rather like a dog waging war against its own tail — and, unfortunately for Sam, his head appeared to have the upper ground. He rocked back and forth like a madman, his hands held to the side of his head like he was in abject turmoil.

"Yes!" he said as the wig finally gave way. Sam had two clumps of hair in his hands, but, to his horror, discovered that the wig was still in situ, albeit now with a patch of hair missing from it. The glue Sam used was stronger than he'd suspected. In his haste to secure the wig in the first place, some of the residual, sticky substance had remained on his palms and now, as it turned out, fused hair directly to them. As such, he was starting to look like a pre-pubescent Chewbacca, and, in fact, he let out a very Wookiee-like groan.

His scalp was starting to burn, and his situation was getting more desperate. His eyes darted around the car looking for something to pry the wig away from his head, but there was nothing obvious. He rummaged around the glove compartment. "*Ah-ha*," he said, gratefully clapping eyes on a large plastic ruler.

His hairy palms, unfortunately, meant that purchase was challenging, and the ruler slid through his grasp every time he tried to use it to prise the wig loose. After several failed attempts — and the formation of a graze on his forehead — he was eventually able to secure a firm hold on the device. He wiggled the ruler and used a sawing action to cut the fabric free from the skin.

The ruler moved relatively freely for a moment or two — and Sam gave a sigh of relief — but then it felt like he was stirring treacle as the glue claimed its second victim. The ruler wouldn't shift and stuck firm. "Fudge!" Sam cursed.

He heard a dog bark in the distance and felt a moment of déjà vu, praying that the woman from the previous encounter was not out on her daily walk. The car door opened right at that moment, startling Sam and causing him to nearly snap the ruler still in his hand.

"I've found the house," announced Abby, climbing back into the car. She looked at Sam's head... down to his hairy hands... and back up to his head. "Seriously, Sam?" was all she could manage, and her eyes drew up to the wig's fresh bald patch.

Sam held out his hands to her to reveal where the hair had ended up. "It's stuck," he said miserably.

Abby put her hand to her cheek. "Oh my," she said calmly, before raising the tone of her voice once again. "Sam! You do know you've got a ruler sticking out the front of your head? You look like a Dalek! A bloody Dalek with alopecia!" The more she spoke, the stronger her voice became, like a steam train gaining speed as its fire was stoked. "Now come here!" she ordered.

Sam did as he was told, and, with her favourable angle and a bit of leverage, Abby was able to rip the ruler loose. But the scream that Sam produced would remain with her for a long time, and she dared go no further.

"You'll have to wear my baseball cap," she insisted.

"But it's pink," Sam protested.

"I don't care what colour it is. If you think I'm breaking into a house on my own, you're very much mistaken. And there's no way we're breaking in with you looking like that."

Sam had panic in his voice. "We're breaking in?"

Abby nodded her head. "Indeed we are. So come on, Teen Wolf, and let's see what we're up against."

A gullible neighbour, or perhaps someone who just wanted Abby off their porch, had confirmed that one of the houses was regularly leased out on a short-term let.

"This is it," said Abby after they'd walked a short distance. It was three doors down from the house that Sam had previously entered in error. "The neighbour thought it was being used as a brothel," Abby carried on. "Until she learned from the owner that it was being rented out on Airbnb. Most importantly, she said she's seen a well-dressed woman, and a man who looked like he'd got lost on a fox hunt."

"Fox hunting is cruel," Sam interjected.

"They've been here for a few days," Abby stated, ignoring the interruption. "Come on," she said, walking up the path like she owned the place.

"What are you doing? We should sneak in the back, surely?" said Sam.

Abby shook her head. "No. I'll knock on the door, and I've got a funny feeling that nobody's going to be in."

Sam shuffled uneasily, attempting to pull the pink cap further over the wig, as Abby rattled the substantial door knocker. Several more attempts and it was clear the house was, in fact, unoccupied.

"Can you pick a lock?" asked Abby.

"What? Of course I can't pick a lock, can you?"

"Well, no. Let's go round the back and see if there's either an open window or a door we can kick in."

Sam's jaw dropped. "What? We can't break in, we'll end up in jail!"

"I *told* you we were breaking in," Abby replied.

"Yes, but when you said break in, I didn't know you meant actually break in!"

"We need to get in that house, it's our only hope," she told him. "You stay here, and shout if you see anything."

"But Abby!" Sam objected, but it was too late as she had already left him.

He scanned the street for activity, but it was quiet. He looked suspiciously at the garden gnome staring up at him from the front garden, with its smugly cheerful grin, and had a flashback to falling in the neighbour's pond. "Little red-hatted bastards," he said, kicking out.

He didn't mean to catch it as truly as he did, and the gnome's head came clean off. "Oh dear, now I've gone and done it," he said, stooping down to see if he could perform life-saving surgery. "If only I had some glue!" he remarked, chuckling to himself.

He lifted the gnome's headless torso and, there, on the ground where it had sat, a little silver wonder sparkled in the sun. "Well, hello, my little beauty," spoke Sam lovingly. It wasn't just him that was stupid enough to hide the front door key under a garden ornament, it seemed, and he was happy for it.

At the front door now, he took a quick look over his shoulder, and then gingerly pushed the key into the lock. In a glorious instant, the mechanism slid, and he pushed the door open.

"Hello, maintenance man!" he shouted, in case he needed a motive for being there — though not that any idiot would believe his credentials. Satisfied, he closed the door behind him and made his way into the lounge. There were two cups sat on the coffee table.

He stopped in his tracks when he heard a groaning noise, and for a moment thought the occupants were upstairs, perhaps enjoying each other's company to put it politely. He heard it again, and every fibre in his body was telling him to retreat, but he pressed on. The noise was coming from the kitchen.

"Maintenance man?" he repeated, more tentatively this time, as he padded over and poked his head through the kitchen door.

There was a grunt now, as he stepped into the kitchen. It was close. Too close. Sam's muscles — what there were of them — tensed, ready to spring to action. "Oof!" came the response. Sam spun round on his heel, towards the sound of certain peril, to face the threat. He had to. For Abby's sake, he *had* to.

"Abby?" Sam called out in a reedy timbre, with nerves apparent in his voice. "Abby, what the hell are you doing?"

Abby had the top half of her body dangling through the kitchen window, with her bottom half hanging precariously out of the other side. "I'm stuck!" she said desperately. "Help me, will you?" she pleaded.

Sam didn't need to be asked twice as he darted to her assistance. He nestled his head into her neck and put his hand under her armpits. "Get ready," he said, as he began to apply pressure. "This might hurt a little."

She was stuck — like the ruler, earlier — but eased gradually through.

"Ow," she said. "Hang on, my trousers are catching on something."

But there was no going back, as Sam struggled under the increasing weight.

"My trousers are being pulled off," said Abby frantically. "You need to stop. Sam, you need to stop!"

"I can't bloody stop, you weigh a ton, I need to get you through!"

"I weigh a ton, do I?"

"Not now, Abby! Let's just agree I always say the wrong thing, right? I've got to... *urmph*... just hang in there, I've got to..."

Every inch Abby progressed saw her trousers pulled down lower. Eventually, she hung down low enough to use her hands to somewhat support herself on the kitchen worktop. By this time, however, her trousers were now by her ankles and her ankles were still by the window opening.

"Sam, you need to unhook my trousers from the window," she said with her arms starting to quiver under the strain. "And if you look at my arse, I'll bloody kill you."

Sam stepped up, and he wrestled with her trousers — which finally came free after a bit of fussing, as it was just a matter of attacking them from the proper position. Sam helped her into the kitchen, and, once standing, she immediately reached down to pull her trousers back up.

Once she'd got herself back together, she pointed a finger at Sam. "Were you faffing about just so you could get a look at my bum?" she demanded.

"No! Of course not!" Sam protested. *Well, maybe a little*, he thought to himself.

Abby continued to adjust herself, pulling on the waist of her trousers while wiggling her hips. "This'll never feel right again. Dammit," she said. "Wait. Hang on a second," she added, abandoning the battle with her trousers. "How the hell is it that you're in the kitchen??"

Sam smiled. "There was a key hidden under the gnome."

"What, people still actually do that?" she answered, before going quiet for a moment.

Sam shifted nervously from foot to foot. He didn't like it when Abby wasn't talking. In his experience, if a woman suddenly went quiet, it meant he was likely to be shouted at shortly thereafter.

"So why didn't you come and tell me before I tried to get through the window??" she shouted at him.

Sam didn't respond. He was trying to think of a response that wouldn't make her angry. He was trying to think... but nothing was happening.

"Are you still thinking about my knickers?" Abby demanded.

It was as if she could read minds!

"A little bit, yes," Sam admitted, casting his eyes down to the floor. "I mean, only a little. I promise."

"There's two cups in the lounge," he said, deftly changing the subject. "And from the look of this kitchen, the people who left had every intention of returning. Let's split up. You take upstairs and I'll do down."

Sam felt every inch the intrepid investigator as he diligently lifted items with his pen so as to preserve any forensic details intact. He had no plan what to do with those items afterwards, but he knew Abby would be impressed if she saw him doing it. He worked methodically through the kitchen, lounge, and the downstairs toilet — although the latter was rather out of necessity.

Once he'd determined the downstairs loo was in full working order — for scientific purposes, of course — he was about to shout to Abby to see if there was anything of interest upstairs when he remembered he'd seen a garage earlier and thought it best to check it out.

The garage door was concealed at the rear of the utility room. Sam listened to the door for a moment — it felt like the right thing to do — before easing the door open. It was dark as he fumbled around, unsuccessfully, for a light switch. The only illumination came from that penetrating the frame of the larger garage door. He could just make out a table and chair in the middle of the floor as he reached for his phone to light the way.

"Where's the bloody light switch?" he called into the darkness, getting frustrated. "Ah," he said, satisfied, in reference to the murky outline of a dangling object on the wall, certain it was a light fixture. He reached for it and tugged on it, fully expecting to be bathed in luminosity... but it was attached to a solid item, further up, rather than a light bulb, and it crashed to the floor.

It was heavy and made quite a commotion as it hit the concrete surface, resulting in the flapping of wings from outside as nearby birds took flight in distress — as well as the cry of a bird, very near, apparently trapped inside the garage.

"Underpants!" Sam screamed at the noise. He didn't usually use *underpants* as a curse word, but it was the first thing that came to mind for some reason.

He jumped back, holding his hands behind him to guide the way, but he made contact with glass jars sat on top of a table — until confronted with the likes of Sam, at least — jars that promptly smashed to the floor, sousing him in some sort of liquid in the process.

Abby put her head around the door, assuming Sam had been murdered. "Sam..." she probed gently. "Are you okay?"

"I'm fine, I think," Sam answered. "But, for the life of me, I cannot find a—"

In a split second, Abby had located the light switch and she looked at him oddly, as he'd removed his pink baseball cap and she'd forgotten for a moment about the violated wig stuck to his scalp underneath. She sighed.

"You're covered in paint," she said, matter-of-factly, as if nothing he did could surprise her any longer. "And your trousers look like a Jackson Pollock composition."

Sam examined himself. "Er... I meant to do this?" he offered hopelessly. "Bollocks," he said. "And these were my good jeans as well."

Despite the state he was in, Sam was intrigued as to what had dropped to the floor, and he picked up the shattered remains — which continued to make the sound of a muzzled bird.

"It's a cuckoo clock?" he said, baffled. "Why would a cuckoo clock be attached to the wall of a virtually empty garage?"

Abby's attention was focussed on the table. "Well it must be Emma Hopkins that stayed here. Or is staying here. These are art supplies. She must have been using this for an art studio."

"It's a bit pants, though, isn't it? Asked Sam. "An international art dealer and artist using a crappy garage like this for a studio? It hardly makes sense."

"There's lots of things here that don't make an awful lot of sense," said Abby, staring directly at Sam as she did so.

Abby picked up a brochure from the table and wiped the excess paint off using Sam's jeans.

Sam gave her a look.

Abby gave him a look right back, which won out over Sam's look. "Oh, they're covered in paint already," she scolded him. "Now look at this," she said, flicking through the pages. "It's for an auction in Switzerland next week."

"So?" said Sam, already occupied by trying to rescue his jeans.

Abby paused for a moment. "Does that clock you've just destroyed look anything like this one?" she asked, thrusting the page in his face.

Now, Sam wasn't stupid. Not entirely, at least. So he knew it wouldn't be in an auction catalogue unless it was worth a few quid. He held the front of the clock in his hand and looked at it, then over to the catalogue, and then back again to the clock.

"Underpants," he said. "That's the one, alright."

Abby went quiet as she skimmed the description. "Sam," she said suddenly. "That clock has an auction estimate of *three-hundred-thousand pounds*."

"Shut the front door!" Sam exclaimed. "That can't be right. Something like that, worth that, is not going to be on the wall of a dusty old garage in the Isle of Man. No chance. Something is fishy here."

Abby didn't reply, as she was in agreement.

"Come on, let's see what else is in here. You check those boxes," Sam suggested, pointing to a stack in the corner.

Sam looked through the desk drawers — with a bit more restraint — carefully avoiding the paint which was dripping onto the floor. He pulled out an exquisite wooden box with a gold latch. He held it at arm's length — illogically thinking it may contain an explosive device (one can never be too careful) — and flicked open the ornate clasp. The interior was as impressive as the exterior, draped in luxurious green velvet. Satisfied it wasn't a bomb, he placed it on a dry patch of the desk. Then something else caught his attention.

"Abby, can you confirm to me that the priceless Viking cross that sold for over a million pounds... actually sold?"

"What? Yes, of course. Why?" she replied.

"Well, I'm no Hugh Scully from *Antiques Roadshow*, but unless I'm very much mistaken it would appear, then, that there are *two* of those unique, priceless Viking crosses... with the other sat in that box, just there. And which is yards away from yet another priceless artefact."

"And another!" said Abby, unrolling a large canvass sheet. "I'm pretty sure that this is the painting Mr Justus has been so eager to retrieve."

"That's it indeed," Sam confirmed. "Bloody hell, Abby, that's worth seventy-five thousand to us!"

"It would," said Abby, rather deflated. "But I don't think Mr Justus is going to be overly ecstatic when he realises that his priceless painting is not alone."

"How do you mean? Asked Sam.

Abby unrolled another canvas. "Well, his priceless painting has a twin brother."

"That's exactly the same as the other one!" said Sam. "No wonder Emma is so rich if she's managed to get her hands on all of these priceless works of art."

Abby rolled her eyes. "Sam, I don't think Emma Hopkins acquired these items. I think Emma Hopkins has been using her unquestionable talent for nefarious means. The talented artist is actually a talented art forger! Now, come on, we need to get this painting to Mr Justus, get paid, and you can turn the whole lot over to your friends at the FBI."

"I don't think Mr Justus is going to pay us when he sees the other painting, exactly the same."

"What other painting? Asked Abby.

"The one we've just... ah, okay," replied Sam, getting the picture. "Wait, but how do we know which to give him? Which one is the original? Or are they both fakes, and the original is still hidden away somewhere?"

"We'll hand that painting over in good faith. If the FBI should stumble across the other one, well, that's Emma's problem, not ours," Abby answered.

"Hang on, but which one do we give him? You haven't answered my question," Sam protested.

"That's your purview, as you're the art expert. At least as far as abstract expressionism is concerned," replied Abby, glancing again at his trousers. "Now grab something to set down on my car seat so you don't create another masterpiece on my upholstery."

Sam reengaged his master disguise (which was actually two disguises in one — the pink hat, which in turn covered up the wig — and now incorporating a third disguise as well in the form of a housepainter, by virtue of his paint-splattered trousers) as they jumped back in the car and drove away with a four-million-pound priceless artwork (or not) rolled up on the back seat.

When they were nearly at the end of the road, a head rose from behind the steering wheel of a black Range Rover which had been parked a ways up the street inconspicuously. The driver put a phone to the side of his face. "I've found her friends, Mr Esposito, and I'm following them now," he said. There was a pause, and, then, "Right. Gotcha."

The black Range Rover pulled away from the kerb, and it began a leisurely pursuit.

Chapter Eight
Justus Served

Stop picking the skin or you'll end up with a scar," said Abby.

"But it's sore," replied Sam, sat at his desk with Abby stood over him.

"I can see that," said Abby, giggling as she looked down on a perfectly red patch on his scalp that looked like a massive sunburn. "Now hold still, the moisturiser is quite cold," she said, applying a liberal application.

"*Aaah,*" moaned Sam. "That feels good."

"I'm going to miss working with Lloyd," she told him. "You really are dead from the neck up at times, but you do make me laugh."

"I'm gratified to know I'm of some use to you," replied Sam. "And, perhaps when you're done with my head, you could give my hands a haircut?"

"I enjoyed working on this case, Sam. I'm kinda sad it's over. I mean, when are we going to get involved in something like this again?"

"The money came in?" Sam enquired.

"Sure did, seventy-five-thousand smackers are currently warming the company bank account. The old man is delighted. This keeps me and you in a job for the next year, at least."

"Excellent, I think I'll leave it a few hours before I phone the FBI," Sam answered. "I wonder if Mr Justus will leave it at that now he's got his painting back. Four million quid for a fake painting. Imagine how angry he'd be if he found out."

"You didn't give him the real one?" Abby asked.

"Your guess is as good as mine," said Sam. "I only know abstract expressionism."

Abby nodded as she continued to massage his scalp. "Ooh, we need to make up a case name when we finish one! What do you reckon?" And she stopped for a moment as she pondered this.

"How do you mean? And please carry on, don't stop now," he asked, and then implored.

"Are you enjoying this maybe a little more than you should be??" Abby asked, her suspicions — among other things — aroused.

"What?" asked Sam, looking up and then following her eye-line down to his trousers. "No! I'm enjoying it just the right amount! Precisely the right amount." He coughed. "And that's just my phone in my pocket — you're not that good," he assured her. But she was. And the phone was actually stored safely on the other side.

He adjusted his seating position. "You were saying?"

"Yes, you know, like Sherlock Holmes in the case of the whatever. We should do one. Abby and Sam in the case of the—"

"Why Abby and Sam?" asked Sam.

"What else would it be?"

Sam shrugged his shoulders. "Well it could be *Sam and Abby*. You know. For instance."

"Abby and Sam rolls off the tongue better," she said, correcting him. "But, anyway, it's a cool idea, right? We could put it on our website under the 'Cases Solved' section."

"It'd be pretty lonely," Sam remarked.

"What would?"

"The 'Cases Solved' section. There'd only be just the one."

"I know," said Abby. "But we had a good result with this one, and, with a bit of advertising, we can get some more juicy cases to get our teeth into."

"Yes, but I've got a feeling that this case isn't over," said Sam, self-possessed. "Not quite yet."

"What?" said Abby. "Mr Justus has his painting back, we've been paid. End of!"

"And what about Emma Hopkins?" asked Sam.

"She'll be long gone, I expect. Probably selling dodgy cuckoo clocks in Switzerland. The Isle of Man will be a distant memory for her."

"Abby," Sam replied, leaning forward as if he had something very grave to relate. "Emma Hopkins is looking at me through the front window."

"You're done," announced Abby. "And don't be daft, she can't possibly…" she began, drying her hands on a tea towel to clean off the last bits of excess moisturiser. And, then, "Oh. She is," she said, as the bell tinkled as the front door opened and Emma stepped in.

"The game is afoot," said Sam.

"What if she's armed, and come to even the score with us for handing the painting back?" Abby whispered. "What'll we do?"

"She wouldn't know, would she? Unless she's spoken to Mr Justus," Sam responded.

"Well, go and attend to her and find out, then," said Abby, taking a cautious step back and clearing the way for Sam.

Sam couldn't look Abby in the eye. "I, em… I probably shouldn't stand up at the moment. It's not a good time for me," he mumbled.

Abby shook her head. "Oh, that'll be the mobile phone again, will it? And by the looks of it, you need to invest in a bigger one. It may be time to upgrade?" she said.

"Hey!" Sam protested. "That's not very—"

"Don't worry," Abby cut in. "I'll take care of this. You'll probably just cock things up anyway," she said, stomping through to the reception area.

"Emma, I thought you'd be long gone by now," said Abby, with just barely hidden contempt, as she attended to Emma.

Emma removed her sunglasses, and it was clear that she was visibly upset. "I don't know where to turn," she said, her voice trembling. "They're going to kill me."

Abby's scorn softened as she stepped aside, allowing Emma to enter the office. "Please come in," she offered.

Sam was now unobstructed and able to stand. "You've met Sam," said Abby. "Please, take a seat."

Emma couldn't take her eyes off Sam's red, raw head — which was in its current state glistening due to the sun coming through the window and reflecting off his heavily moisturised bonce.

"It's glue. From my wig," explained Sam, attempting to maintain a tone that said this was all perfectly normal and not at all cause for concern.

Emma, decorum intact, extended her hand to Sam.

"I can't," said Sam. "Can't shake your hand, that is. My hands are, well…" he said, trailing off, waving one of his hands in a *these-aren't-the-droids-you're-looking-for* type of flourish.

Emma's nerves were not being settled by her introduction to Sam, from the expression on her face, and it appeared as if she were uncertain she'd come to the right place seeking help. She looked at Abby for assurance, like you'd do with a dog owner to make sure their very-questionable-looking pet was of a safe enough disposition to approach.

"Also, from the wig," explained Sam, again, as if this were not at all unusual.

"Anyway…" said Abby. "I must admit that we're a little surprised to see you here."

Emma had her hair tied back tightly and looked exhausted, with black circles under her eyes. "I need your help to get off this island," she said, drained.

"We're not exactly travel agents?" said Sam, not unsympathetically.

"I know," replied Emma. "But I don't know what else to do."

"Could you not, say, forge a plane ticket?" asked Abby, with slightly less sympathy than Sam.

Emma's head dropped. "Ah. You know about that, then."

"Yes," Sam confirmed. "We had the pleasure of seeing your temporary art studio."

"Shit! You were at the house I was renting?" she asked.

Sam nodded, startled at the sudden vulgarity. "Yes, and we saw your handiwork."

Emma pressed her hand against her forehead. "Mr Esposito has had someone watching the house. If they saw you, and I'm sure they must have, then I'm afraid the both of you are in danger now also."

"Okay," responded Abby flatly, unsure she believed Emma to be telling the truth. "But don't you mean Mr Justus?"

"No. Mr Esposito. Mr Justus is a nasty piece of work, but compared to Esposito he's like a kitten."

"Mr Justus is gone, at least," explained Sam. "All he wanted was his painting, so he's out of the picture now."

"Please tell me you didn't give him the painting??" asked Emma, panicked.

Sam looked at Abby and then back to Emma. "Yes," he said. "It was his, after all?"

Emma stood. "Did you see there were two paintings almost exactly the same? Which one did you give him?" she asked desperately, darting her eyes back and forth between the two of them.

"Sam?" Abby deferred.

Sam tried to think. "They were the same... I don't know, em..."

Emma slapped her hand on the desk, hard, startling Sam out of his wits. "Did you give him the one that was in the crate or the one near the table??" she demanded.

Sam pulled his thoughts together. "The one... to the left? In the crate. Why?"

"Oh, no!" Emma exclaimed.

"What?" Sam asked, confused. "Was that the real one?"

"No," she explained. "The original of that painting is somewhere in Japan in a private collection. We chose to copy that one because we knew it was unlikely to ever be seen publicly, but I made a mistake when I was copying it. We'd already taken his money when I realised that one of the shades I'd used wasn't exactly right. I couldn't hand it over, so I had to go into hiding until I'd had a chance to fix it. Or make another one."

"Wait, so they were *both* fakes?" asked Sam, trying to work it all out. "And I gave him the wrong fake?"

"Yes. And because I went into hiding, he had already thought I'd stolen his money. But now—"

"Well you have, technically," interrupted Sam. "Stolen his money, I mean. Any way you look at it. Right? I mean, you've sold him a painting that's worth what, fifty pounds, either way? For over four million. That's not a bad day's work. You must have made an absolute fortune from ripping people off. We know you sell coun-terfeit paintings and Viking crosses. What else is there?"

"Don't forget the cuckoo clocks!" said Abby.

"Oh yes, the clocks," said Sam. "Oh, by the way, I think I broke your clock. Sorry. I suppose you can just make another one?"

Emma's eyes glazed over, and her bottom lip trembled like jelly a millisecond before the waterworks arrived. "I didn't mean to get in this mess," she said sporadically between emotional gasps of air. "I wanted out."

Sam's right eyebrow took flight. "You wanted out?" he said. "That's exactly what I said to Abby. Didn't I, Abby? I said — whilst I was walking around your temporary art gallery — *this looks like someone who's retiring from the forgery business.*"

Emma's shoulders convulsed as the tears flowed freely, and Sam knew from the look he'd just received from Abby that it was time to let up.

"Take a seat," offered Abby. "Can I get you a drink of water?" she offered, relaxing the mood in the room. She gave Emma a moment to compose herself before contin-uing. "Emma, you can understand why sympathy is a bit thin on the ground? How do you mean you wanted out?" she asked.

Emma gave Sam a half-smile as she took a sip from the plastic cup of water he handed her. "I wanted out," she said. "But, unfortunately, Mr Esposito had other ideas."

Sam exhaled in frustration. "You're going to have to help us out here, Emma. Who exactly is he, and who is Mr Justus? Also, since when did people think it was ac-ceptable to call themselves Mister such-and-such? If I all-of-a-sudden announced my name as Mr Levy, eve-ryone would take the piss. Abby, you'd take the piss?" he asked.

"Absolutely," replied Abby.

"You can call yourself Mister," replied Emma. "When you're a sadistic psychopath?"

Sam screwed up his eyes as if considering this to be an option. "Carry on," he requested.

"Mr Esposito is a gangster," explained Emma. "If you met him in the street, you might think he was harmless. But trust me. He isn't. He's involved in organised crime all over the world."

"Including forgery?" asked Sam.

"Including forgery," said Emma, taking a further sip of water. "You only have to look at the money for that Viking cross, or the painting for Mr Justus. It's easy to see why Mr Esposito is involved, and why he was so up-set when I told him I wanted out. I said I'd complete the last few jobs for him, and he gave me the impression that I was retiring with his blessing. That is, until I re-ceived word that he might not be as pleased to see the back of me as I'd hoped."

"So, do we know who Mr Justus is yet?" asked Sam, glancing towards Abby, and then back to Emma. "How's he involved in this? Innocent victim?"

"Good god, no!" replied Emma. "Mr Justus is just stu-pid and very, very greedy. He's been buying artwork off Mr Esposito for years. Only, with this one, as I said, I made a mistake. A mistake he'd have picked up on in an instant. He's not stupid in that respect."

Sam nodded, but he still didn't really have a clue. "Why the hell has he been buying fake paintings for years?"

"He... doesn't exactly know they're fake," Emma re-plied. "As I said a moment ago, I only ever forge art-works which are never likely to come into the view of the general public. Mr Esposito tells me what to forge, and he arranges the sale. In the case of Mr Justus, he was told the paintings he was buying were stolen, which is why he would then buy them at a significant discount. And then, presumably, sell them on and make an enormous profit. So, stupid and greedy. And with the continued demand, Mr Esposito must have decided that it was too much of a business risk to let me go."

"How did you end up involved with someone like him?" asked Abby.

Emma's body deflated. "I was — well, still am — a good artist. He bought a couple of my paintings from an exhibition. I had no idea what he was or what he did. We met socially a couple of times, and he was, well, charming. I met him several times more in situations that, unbeknown to me, he'd engineered. I mentioned that I'd always wanted to own my own gallery, and before I knew it he was handing me the keys to my own business in London. He asked me to copy a picture for him, which I did. And another and another. I suppose I was naïve or turned a blind eye. Either way, the business expanded into other galleries all over the world. Before long, I was in too deep. And as if this situation couldn't get much worse, Mr Justus will now know that the painting he's in possession off is a fake, and it won't take a genius to figure out he's been buying fakes for years."

Emma looked at them solemnly. "They will kill me if they catch me. And I don't mean to drop you guys right into it. But if the house has been watched, then, well, you're kind of now in this mess along with me."

Sam's cheeks flushed. "You cheeky bi–"

"Sam," Abby admonished, holding her index finger aloft.

"What?" Sam protested. "I was going to say *biscuit.*"

"Anyway, she's got a point," Abby told him. "Neither of these two, oh, *Mr Men,* I think I'm going to start calling them—"

"That could get confusing," interrupted Sam, knocking Abby off her stride.

"What could?" she asked, slightly put out.

"The Mr Men. What about *Mr J* and *Mr E?*"

"But that's not funny," said Abby. "Whereas Mr Men is funny because it's a book."

"No, but think," Sam replied. "Mr E. *Mystery*. Ha! It's good, right?"

"Right," replied Abby, though unconvinced. "Emma," she asked. "Which one do you like? Mr Men? Or Mr J and Mr E?"

Emma looked pained, "I've got two psychopaths trying to kill me and you think I care about what I should call them??" She stared at Sam and Abby like a parent chastising a child that'd been caught shoplifting.

"I thought mine was clever," Sam moaned, looking down at the floor.

Emma realised that these two, Sam and Abby, were pretty much her only hope at this point. She inhaled deeply. "Abby's," she let out as she exhaled. "Let's go with Mr Men, I suppose. I don't know the book. But it's easier to say."

Sam shuffled his feet, moping.

Abby flicked her head in victory, giving Sam a smug look, her eyes half-closed like a sniper taking aim.

Abby turned back to Emma. "Why don't we just hand you over to the police?" she said, matter-of-fact.

Emma took her head in her hands. "You think this is about *me?*" she said in disbelief. "I don't care about the police, I'm *working* with the police," she continued. "Well, the FBI, that is," she added.

Sam had a puzzled expression, as if someone had farted, and he was trying to work out from whence the bottom-burp had emanated. "The... the FBI?" he said, innocently.

"Yes," replied Emma. "They were my ticket out of this entire fiasco. I work for them and get evidence against...

Mr Men… and they let me go. Well, that was the plan, anyway. Until they inform me that Mr Esposito has taken my sister hostage. If I go back to the FBI, he'd think nothing of hurting my sister."

Sam continued his pose of sniffing the air. "The FBI?" he repeated. "The FBI, you say?"

"What do you want from us?" asked Abby. "We can't get you off the island, and we're certainly not going up against the bleedin' Mafia on your behalf."

"I just need a bit of time. I need to think. I need to sleep. Once I've got a clear head, I'll figure out what to do. I can sleep here, on the floor," she said, pointing, as if they didn't know where the floor was.

Abby looked at Sam. "Sam. The old man's holiday home. Have you still got the key?"

"Yeees…" replied Sam with great uncertainty. "But that's only in case of emergency. He'll go nuts if we—"

"This would qualify as an emergency," she said, once again cutting him off with a swipe of the index finger. "Emma, you can stay there," Abby asserted. "I know it's empty at the moment. It's in the middle of nowhere. You'll be safe for a few days."

Emma's eyes were red and puffy from crying, "Thank you," she responded. "Thank you so much. I need to figure out how to keep my sister safe. She has nothing to do with this… this mess," she said, her voice cracking with emotion.

For someone eager to distance themselves from this sordid affair, even Sam surprised himself when he announced, "I'll help you find your sister." He swelled out his chest, like a cheap superhero. All that was missing was a flick of the cape.

It was now Abby's turn to take on the role of the fart sniffer, and snarled at Sam, *"We* will help her find—"

"That's right, Abby." And, positions reversed, Sam was now the one to flick his index finger. He then continued on, like Gotham's finest, fists clenched, back arched, and with his chin proudly elevated. "Never fear, Emma. My associate and I shall indeed come to your aid." And, turning back to his 'associate', he said, "Abby, you wanted another case to put on the website? Well, we'll soon be able to put on *The Case of the Missing Sister.*"

"That's a rubbish name," said Abby, dowsing Sam's flames of vigour. "Promise me one thing?" she asked.

"Anything," said Sam.

"Promise me you'll get another wig. I really enjoyed working with Lloyd," she said, smiling broadly.

Chapter Nine
Watching You Watching Me

Laxey in the Isle of Man was stunning. A tranquil village in the east of the isle which boasted a considerable heritage in the island's former mining industry, it is also home to the world's largest working waterwheel as well as a main hub on the electric railway. With a glorious beach and spectacular views, it remains a destination of choice for tourists trying to recapture a sense of nostalgia, and, perhaps, an ice cream while absorbing the glorious Manx countryside. It was an obvious destination to own a holiday home to cater for the enthusiastic tourist trade, but, today, a chocolate-box cottage tucked away in this pretty little village was host to one of the most prolific and successful art forgers currently in operation.

With Emma safely dispatched — for now — at the holiday cottage in Laxey, Abby drove up the narrow roads, roads clearly designed for a time where the motorcar was a distant and unforeseen consideration. She pulled to a gentle stop as crossing lights flashed red, and a moment later an electric tram passed in front of them. Abby smiled, as she spied a small child on the tram — her face pressed to the glass — waving at the waiting traffic.

"Aw, I used to always do that," Abby said warmly, waving back and using two hands for full effect, until another child — likely the little girl's brother — pushed his way into view and extended his middle finger in Abby's direction.

"Little tosser!" said Sam, sticking his head out of the window closely followed by his extended arm with a backwards victory sign held firmly aloft.

"Sam!" said Abby, trying to stifle laughter. "I've never seen you like this! What's got into you? And you can't do that!"

"Can and did," Sam replied, chin held up, and unrepentant.

"I bet you were just like that little boy when you were small. You know. Doing what he just did."

"Rubbish!" Sam insisted. "I came into this world fully grown!"

Abby shook her head, laughing, as the tram passed in front of them on its coastal journey towards Douglas. Once clear, she shifted into gear and reengaged in their own journey.

"Something's on your mind," Abby said, serious now once they'd been on their way for a bit, looking over at Sam.

"What? No," Sam answered.

"There is. I can tell by the way you breathe," she told him.

"By the way I breathe?" scoffed Sam. "There's only one way to breathe, I'll have you know, and that's in and out. And even I can manage that most times."

"When you're thinking — really hard — you slow your breathing, like you've forgotten how, and then take in a really big lungful. So, I can tell you've got something on your mind."

"According to you," Sam replied, defiant, like a little boy got caught dead-to-rights picking his nose but denying it anyway.

"I know you, Sam," Abby continued. "You do it when you're doing something mentally taxing — for you, like a crossword, or, say, tying your shoelaces."

"That shoelace knot is tricky, it's not my fault!" Sam replied, and they both had a laugh. After a quiet pause, however, Sam confided softly, "It's true, though. Look, I think I have made a bit of a mistake," he said, his head bowed.

"You mean about the shorts you're wearing?" Abby replied. "I kinda agree, they're a bit... neat."

Sam looked wounded. "No, not my shorts. That's the fashion," he insisted. "Abby, I'm being serious now. As I said, I think I might have made a little mistake."

"Do I need to guess? Because I'm a good guesser," Abby came back.

Sam was only half paying attention to her teasing, and so misheard 'guesser' as *kisser*. It took him a moment to realise his mistake before carrying on.

"Right. Sooo," said Sam in a drawn-out manner before getting to the point. "You know when I said to Emma that the painting I gave to Mr Justus' people..."

"Yes...?" Abby replied expectantly.

"Weeeell... I may have said it was the one from the crate?"

"Yes...?" Abby replied expectantly yet again. Then she abruptly switched off the car radio. "Wait," she said. "You mean that's not the one you actually gave her? That's more than a little mistake, Sam!" she shouted.

Sam, for his part, recoiled like the head of a startled tortoise.

"Are you going to tell me that you gave the correct one, and that poor woman thinks a crazed lunatic is trying to kill her because you made a little mistake??"

"No," he offered, unconvincingly. "Okay, I think so. Well, I know so. It's good news that at least there's one less crackpot trying to hunt her down, no?" he said trying to create a positive spin.

Abby's fingers clattered on the steering wheel like a team of horses' hooves. "I suppose so," she finally conceded. "I could throttle you at times, Sam Levy," she added. "But if Mr Justus has truly buggered off, then we only have to worry about this other nutjob. This Mr Esposito."

Abby continued to tap her finger on the steering wheel as they drove along, but the clattering at least was reduced to the sound of one horse as opposed to a team of horses.

Sam wasn't comfortable with awkward silence — but went with it, taking the opportunity to soak in the vibrant green countryside of which there was an abundance on this glorious, sun-kissed afternoon. His mind was working overtime, and, as such, he tried to regulate his breathing for fear of passing out.

"You weren't being serious, were you?" he eventually asked, hesitantly.

"About throttling you?" confirmed Abby.

"No, about the shorts. I thought I carried them off quite well."

"Sam, they looked like they're painted on you. I'm sure you could almost see your…" she said, unwilling to complete the thought aloud.

It went quiet again, but not awkward. Well, at least not on Sam's part — he was just biding his time…

"So. You were, eh, looking at what the big dog has got tucked away, down there, were you?"

Abby had predicted the protracted response was coming, but she couldn't prevent a tinge of rouge caressing her cheeks nevertheless. "It was hard to miss," was her reply.

Sam nodded happily, pleased as punch. "Thanks!" he said, fit to burst.

"That wasn't a compliment!" countered Abby, deflating Sam's pride. "Rather a reflection on how tight your shorts are."

Sam held his gaze for a moment longer than usual, and he looked at her carefully. Abby was a little too short for the driving position, he observed. When she pressed the clutch, it was as if she needed blocks on the end of her shoes; her nose was all but pressed against the windscreen. He was a PI, after all; he noticed things.

"I can see you watching me," said Abby. "Out of the corner of my eye. Are you going to say something about the way I drive?"

Sam smiled. There was no logic for the timing of his current thought process, and, on reflection — in view of the present hostage situation and criminal intent, especially — he thought it ill-advised to share what was on his mind. But it'd been bouncing around in his brain, anxious to be released.

He pressed his fingernails into the palms of his hand and bit the inside of his lip. He bobbed his head as his inner turmoil was reaching a crescendo — it was now or never.

"Abby," he said tentatively, clearing his throat in the process. He waited for a response, but it was not forthcoming.

"Abby," he said once again. "I've been thinking about something."

"Don't hurt yourself," said Abby, quick as a flash.

The response caught Sam off-guard, and for a moment his confidence levels collapsed like a wet cardboard box. He sat with a heavy heart for a moment until he became aware of the pain in his mouth where the gnawing had drawn blood. He spoke to himself, a stronger part of his psyche giving him confidence; there was a pep talk occurring in his head like a prize-winning fighter about to enter the ring.

"Abby," he ventured once again, but there was no response.

Abby for her part wasn't being rude, at least not intentionally. Sam was whimpering like a petrified vole, and she was simply concentrating on driving (and reaching the pedals).

Sam carried on. "You know how I said I'd take you out to dinner one time? Well, you probably don't, but I did."

Abby's eyes shifted furtively, as Sam continued.

"Well, if it'd be okay. With you, I mean," he said, fumbling with his hands, absently searching for remaining hairs. "I just wondered if you'd like to, you know, go out for something to eat. Together, I mean."

Abby sat bolt upright. "Oh, you have *got* to be kidding me," she said harshly, her voice tinged with anger. "I do *not* need this nonsense right now."

Sam's confidence level had not been terribly high to begin with, despite his internal pep talk. If he'd been a prize-fighter before, he was now sat in the corner, on a small stool, beaten and bruised, a wet towel draped over his head, and Burgess Meredith shouting *"Yer a bum!"* in that gravelly voice of his into Sam's ear.

Sam pressed his head against the window. He was too embarrassed to even look at Abby. He gave a pitiful sigh, and his exhaled breath fogged the cold glass, obscuring his view.

"We're being followed," Abby announced.

Sam barely stirred, until she repeated it once again with even more urgency. He reluctantly turned his head round and was startled by both the appearance of a sleek black car positioned directly behind them, as well as its proximity — millimetres from their rear bumper.

"Maybe they're just trying to get past?" offered Sam, desperately.

"The one in the passenger seat has got a gun – they're not out for an afternoon drive!" shouted Abby. "Phone the police! Now!"

Sam patted himself over frantically. "Bollocks! My phone's in my coat. Which is in the boot of the car."

Abby's voice was now shrill and at a pitch that would cause audible injury to canines in the vicinity. "What the hell is it doing there!" she screamed. "It's of no use to us there!"

Sam was proper panicked, looking over his shoulder at the man now indicating, with his gun, that they should pull over to the side of the road.

"It's the shorts, Abby!" he shouted back. "My phone didn't fit in the pocket because they were too tight!"

"What did I tell you!" Abby yelled back.

"Oh, blast these bleeding shorts!" Sam exclaimed. And, then, "You're going to have to speed up, try and outrun them!" he instructed, ever helpful.

Abby's face was even closer to the steering wheel than usual as she flicked her attention between the road ahead and the looming image in her rear-view mirror.

"Speed up!" insisted Sam again, which likely only served to increase her anxiety levels.

"Sam!" she shouted. "It's a bloody Ford Focus, not a Porsche!"

Sam gripped onto the side of his seat as Abby threw the car into a sharp left-hand bend. "It's a Ford Fiesta, not a Focus," he said, correcting her through gritted teeth.

"I don't care what it is!" replied Abby. "Unless this car has a set of wings and a jet engine stuck to the roof, we're not going to outrun them. My phone is in my handbag on the parcel shelf. You'll need to reach over and..."

Sam opened one eye and immediately felt a searing pain running down the left side of his face. "Ahhh," he groaned. He spluttered as the blood which ran down his cheek ran freely into his mouth. His vision was blurry, and it took a minute or two for things to sharpen back into focus.

It took a further moment before he could work out where he was and what had happened. "Abby, are you okay?" he asked, once he'd recovered his senses. "Abby," he repeated. "Are you okay?" He looked to the driver's seat, but it was empty. "Abby!" he said once again, only louder.

She was gone, but the engine was still running. The car had spun 180 degrees on the narrow country lane, with Sam's door now pressed firmly up against a grass bank. The driver's door was partly ajar, so he took off his seatbelt and shimmied over, taking the opportunity to examine his injury in the rear-view mirror as he did so. Aside from a discoloured egg-shaped lump on the side of his head and a small gash — under his eye, where the blood had originated — he was in fairly good shape, it seemed, although more pain was sure to present itself later on.

He got out of the car to see if Abby was nearby, injured. But there was no sign of her. He put his hand to his head once again. "I wonder how long I was out," he said to himself. He scanned the narrow road, both ways, but she simply wasn't there. "Abby!" he screamed. "Where are you??"

He sat on the bonnet of the car, head in his hands. "Bollocks!" he said aloud. "Abby!"

He examined the car for damage, but, like his head, it appeared mainly superficial. The two left wheels had come to rest in a narrow ditch, but the car looked to be relatively intact. He climbed into the driver's seat.

"Come on," he pleaded as the wheel struggled to gain traction. He fought with the steering wheel as he applied the accelerator liberally. "Come on, you little bastard," he said, as the car eventually eased itself free.

With no clue as to Abby's whereabouts, Sam sped back on the route they'd just travelled. He knew that those who'd forced them off the road must have known where Emma was holed up.

Sam had started the day tasked with finding one woman — Emma's sister — and it was now looking likely that he was now looking for three women. "Shit, shit, shit," he said, as he sped back toward Laxey, hoping beyond hope that Emma was still safe.

He shifted uncomfortably in his seat, concerned that the pain near his tailbone may be as a result of the car crash. With one hand left on the wheel, he used his free hand to reach down and search for any obvious injury. He was relieved to find that there was, in fact, no apparent injury — just the mother of all wedgies. The impact of the crash, it would appear, had caused his shorts — already too tight — to ride up his back, causing the gusset area to seek shelter halfway up his bum.

"You're going in the soddin' fire, as soon as I get home," he admonished his shorts, whilst wrestling the fabric free from between his two cheeks (though, to be fair, if the shorts had a mind, incineration would very likely have been a decidedly more desirable destination than their current location).

Sam continued to shout expletives, and the horrible realisation sunk in that he might be in the muck much too deep — just like the fabric of his shorts.

"Abby, please be all right," he implored, as he sped — at considerable velocity — passing the sign welcoming "safe drivers" to Laxey.

Chapter Ten
The Pillow Case

I went to college, Mikey, did you know that?" the man said, in a deep, rasping voice with a thick New York accent. When he didn't get a response, he continued. "I wanted to be a vet. Or something with animals. I like animals," he said, stroking the back of his plate-like hand like it were a sick dog. "I used to volunteer at the zoo when I was a kid, back home. I should do that again," He stared out the window with a sense of melancholy. "Mikey, what about you?"

Mikey gripped the steering wheel — his hands enveloped in black leather gloves — and gave his colleague no attention to speak of.

"Mikey?" his partner insisted on asking again.

"What?" said Mikey eventually, with little interest but finally seeing no choice but to acknowledge the question.

"About you. What did you want to do?"

Mikey laughed, in not a laugh-out-loud laugh but rather a resigned I've-accepted-my-lot kind of laugh. "Joey," he said. "I'm not the animal sort. Sure, I like to shoot them. You know. In a field. That sort of thing."

Joey was wounded by his colleague's reply, but he refrained from responding to it. He glanced at the cattle prod protruding from the waistband of his partner's trousers, and he stifled an expression of disdain by momentarily looking out the window. Joey's broad shoulders easily filled the sumptuous leather seat. His neck gathered in folds above the constricting collar of his formal white shirt. He was a hulk of a man, but he was not without feeling.

"What do you tell your wife when you come away on trips like this?" Joey asked, facing his partner again. There was a vulnerability to be found there, on Joey's face, if his partner had known where to look. For a man with a face as weathered and intimidating as Joey had, however, that vulnerability was well hidden.

Mikey threw him a glance. "What?" he said curtly, impatient at this line of questioning. "What the hell are you talking about now?"

"Your wife. What do you tell her?"

"I'm not married," Mikey replied.

"Okay, girlfriend, brother, uncle, what-have-you," Joey offered. "There must be someone you say goodbye to when you go on a trip. What do you say to them?"

"What?" repeated Mikey, with no attempt to hide his displeasure. "I tell them I'm going away. On business."

"Ah," said Joey. "That's my point. What do you tell them? You can't exactly say, I'm a henchman, and I'm going away to kidnap people and attack people with a cattle prod."

Mikey shrugged his shoulders. "I tell them I'm going on business."

"I tried that," said Joey. "But it didn't work. That just prompted more questions. I need some sort of cover story that doesn't promote more questions and that seems plausible."

"Plausible?" said Mikey. "What the hell kind of word is that for a hitman? Christ, you're just like the people on this stupid island — you speak English, but you don't speak English."

"I'm sorry," Joey began. "I didn't realise—"

"The problem with you is, you think too much," Mikey interrupted.

"I... what?" Joey wasn't sure how to even respond.

"That's right. I'm tellin' you, thinking about things too much is the cause of most problems. It only leads to trouble. Believe me, I've given this a lot of thought."

"You've... given this a lot of thought, have you?" asked Joey, somewhat incredulous. "Not too much thought, though, I hope?"

"I can think smart things too!" Mikey insisted, oblivious to the jab. "Just because I never finished school, and just because I don't read books and stuff and know big words like you do, doesn't mean I can't think smart things sometimes!"

"Okay," Joey replied, trying to placate his partner, particularly because it was Mikey who was behind the wheel. "No offence meant."

The drive was very quiet for the next ten minutes or so until, eventually, Joey spoke again.

"So what did you tell them?" he said.

"What?" asked Joey, confused.

"Your wife, girlfriend, or whatever," Mikey replied. "So what did you tell them about what you were doing?"

Mikey had clearly been giving this a lot of thought during the interim. Joey smiled. "Girlfriend," he said. "She likes animals, too."

"Going out with you, that doesn't surprise me," Mikey chuckled.

Joey let the comment pass and responded to Mikey's question. "I told her I'm doing missionary work with the poor," he explained. "But I need to come up with something better."

"Yeah, no kidding, right?" replied Mikey. But then he thought for a moment. "Wait, so she actually *believed* that bullcrap missionary line?"

"Sure," said Joey. "She's—"

"Stupid?" Mikey suggested.

"Trusting," Joey said, correcting him. "She's lovely, and she has no reason to believe I'm lying to her."

Mikey pressed the indicator lever on the steering column and pulled the car off the main road, through an imposing stone entrance gate, and then up a winding tree-lined driveway. The house was impressive, even from the distance of their current vantage point. They were near to the island's airport, and a jet had commenced its final approach noisily above them. The quaint village of Castletown was visible in the distance through a break in the trees where the ancient castle filled the panoramic view.

"I don't understand this," said Joey. "I know Mr Esposito has got a bottomless pit of cash. But how does he just show up virtually unannounced on an island, and yet still manage to get access to a property like this? It's freaking amazing."

"He knows people, I guess?" offered Mikey.

Joey remained unconvinced. "The boss didn't even know the name of the island when we arrived. I just don't get it."

"You don't need to get it, Joey. You just need to do what the boss says, see? This is exactly what I was talking about before."

"I wonder if they go on Airbnb?" Joey mused, more thinking out loud now than talking to his partner.

"What?" responded Mikey, annoyed. He tended to get annoyed when he didn't understand things. Consequently, he was often annoyed.

"Airbnb," Joey repeated, turning to face his associate now. "Do you think they have a specialised section for mob bosses and multinational criminals? I mean, how else do they get property like this, and at such short notice?"

Mikey laughed derisively. It was easier than trying to work out what his partner was on about. "Regardless of how he does it, Joey, our job was to bring Emma Hopkins to him," he said. "So, that means I go home with a big fat bonus check. Which makes me very happy. And I could care less how he got this place."

"*Couldn't* care less," Joey mumbled under his breath, not loud enough to be heard.

"Come on," said Mikey, confident the conversation had been settled. "Get her out of the back. And if she gives you any trouble, I'll introduce her to my cattle prod." He patted his device affectionately.

Joey was a hulk of a man, but he was a gentleman. Well, as gentlemanly as you can possibly be with a woman you've currently got bound, gagged, kidnapped, and with a pillowcase thrown over her head. He opened the rear door and extended a firm but gentle hand. "Out you come," he said gently. "Don't do anything foolish and you'll be just fine."

He helped her out of the car and escorted her over to the impressive white mansion house, pillowcase still in place over her head. "Mikey," he said. "Do you think the boss just sits there on a big throne waiting for us to return? You know, like a Bond villain?" He had to. He just couldn't help himself. The only way to amuse himself on these outings was to get his partner riled up.

Mikey shook his head dismissively. "Hurry up," he simply said in response. "And keep a firm grip on her."

With Emma in tow, Joey bowed his head in acknowledgement to another brutish man stood guard in the vast entrance hall at the front of the house.

"Where's the boss?" asked Mikey, who in return received a grunt and a glance in the direction of a room further up the marble-tiled corridor.

"That's another thing," said Joey, once past the entry guard. "Who's that guy at the door? He didn't come with us on the plane."

"How the hell should I know?" Mikey replied.

"This goes back to my earlier point," Joey reflected. "Mr E has this house on standby, and all of a sudden there's staff all over the place and a thug standing menacingly at the front door. Where do you recruit henchmen?"

"You should know," said Mikey. "He must have hired you just like he hired everybody else."

"Well, yes," Joey replied, using his formidable hand to guide Emma into a quicker pace. "But I used to be a driver. And my position just... sort of evolved."

Mikey stopped and turned. "Joey, you seriously need to stop thinking so much. It will get you killed."

Mikey used the gold sovereign ring on his finger, and rapped on the imposing oak door before entering without invitation.

Mr Esposito sat with his arms resting on an expansive mahogany desk, his face engrossed in a stack of uneven paperwork. He held an antique silver teaspoon and gently stirred a cup of coffee in a delicate china cup, and the scent of Italian dark roast filled the room.

Mr Esposito didn't avert his gaze, but acknowledged those stood in front of him by slowly raising his index finger. It wasn't at first apparent, but aside from attending to the paperwork, Mr Esposito was also hosting a call on speakerphone. He idly drummed his fingertips atop his desk, before saying, "Well, if we cannot buy him. You know what to do." He said this placidly, and yet in a voice that nevertheless sounded menacing.

Joey and Mikey stood, waiting their turn, flanking Emma — who remained gagged and with a cover over her head. She moaned incoherently, stopping only to kick out at the nearest shins she could find. Joey gripped her arm with more force than he had previously and pressed her forward after Mr Esposito ended his call, presenting her to him.

"Very fine," said Mr Esposito softly, looking off the rim of his glasses. "Mr Swan," he added, to no one within view. In an instant, however, Mr Swan appeared from behind a door at the rear corner of the room.

"Would you mind bringing Madeline to me?" Mr Esposito said, addressing Mr Swan, before returning his attention to those stood in front of him once more. "I do enjoy a family reunion, and I am sure Madeline will be delighted to see her sister once again."

Mr Esposito ushered the trio closer with a wiggle of his index finger. "So. Emma Hopkins. We really should not leave you waiting, especially when we have your sister here, who I am certain is quite eager to see you." And, then, "Is that not correct?" he said to Madeline, who had now appeared beside him.

"Was the pillowcase necessary?" asked Mr Esposito to no one in particular.

Joey stepped forward a pace. "Sir. We didn't want her to know where you were staying, sir," he said, his large hands held one over the other in front of him, politely.

"Very fine," said Mr Esposito. "When you are ready," he added, continuing to look at Joey.

Joey did not immediately respond. He was lost in thought, wondering how long Mr Swan had been waiting behind that door before being called upon. He was curious to know how these things worked.

Mikey seized the opportunity, removing the pillowcase, and unfastening the gag from Emma's mouth. Mikey stepped forward now as well, ready to receive the plaudits. He had a dumb smile on his face, and he'd never been properly introduced to manners. "There ya go, Mr E," he said, with unwarranted familiarity.

Mr Esposito took his left hand and flattened his receding white hairline, very slowly, while taking a deep breath. With his right hand, he gently stirred his coffee. The tinkling of the spoon against the china cup made a sound not unlike a ship's bell, marking the time. He then raised his head slightly up, turning it from left to right in a graceful arc, like a silent lion's roar, while he loosened his silk cravat to make himself more comfortable. "Who is this?" Mr Esposito asked evenly, though a vein on his forehead was throbbing noticeably.

With Mikey realising there was no adulation to be had, he immediately stepped back to his former position.

Joey looked at Mikey, and Mikey at Joey. If the two of them weren't currently in such a precarious situation, one could easily be forgiven for assuming they were bashful lovers unsure who was going to make the first move.

"Boss?" asked Mikey tentatively.

"Sir?" asked Joey.

"Who is this?" Mr Esposito repeated.

Joey quickly understood that Mr Esposito would not have asked this previous question if all were well. He took the opportunity to also moisten his lips before speaking again. "Sir? This is Emma Hopkins… sir?" he said, not at all confident in what he was saying as he would have been only a moment before.

Mikey took a further pace back.

"Do I look like a stupid man?" asked Mr Esposito, eerily calm, but the pulsing vein betraying his fury. "Mr Swan," he said, turning to Mr Swan. "Tell me, do I look like a stupid man?"

Mr Swan stepped forward like he was on military parade. "No sir, Mr Esposito, you are many things, but stupid is not one of them."

"Thank you, Mr Swan. Very fine," replied Mr Esposito, before rising from his desk and advancing towards Joey — who now had a shimmering patch of moisture forming on his forehead.

Madeline started to laugh. "Who's that?" she asked.

"Exactly," said Mr Esposito, indulging the impertinent interruption. "Who is this?"

Despite his massive frame, Joey's knees were starting to feel wobbly. "Sir," he said, ever the gentleman. "We followed the car, sir, as instructed. We were told the registration number of the car, where Emma Hopkins was likely to be, and procured this woman from it once an opportunity presented itself."

"Tell me, young lady," said Mr Esposito, now turning to the woman before him for answers. "Would you mind helping us resolve this game of *Guess Who?* If you are not Emma Hopkins, which I know you are not, then who do I have the pleasure of addressing?"

Despite his anger, Mr Esposito was unflappable and he remained in complete control of his faculties.

"My name is Abby," said Abby, acutely aware of the danger her current situation had presented her with. "These two knuckle-dragging Neanderthals took me from my car and gagged me before I could even get a word out."

Joey shifted his weight uncomfortably from one foot to the other. He was sensitive about his looks and didn't like being mistaken for a mug.

Mikey, meanwhile, took the insult in stride. He was used to insults. In fact, insults, he felt, meant he was doing his job well.

"I see," Mr Esposito responded. "And, Miss Abby, how do you fit into this picture, if I may ask?"

"Well..." Abby began, considering her strategy, but then deciding that, under present circumstances, the truth (up to a point, at least) was the wisest course of action. "I'm a private investigator," she said proudly. "And I was originally hired to find Emma Hopkins, and then hired by Emma herself to find out who was trying to find her, and, well... it all got very confusing. Suffice to say, however, I am not Emma Hopkins. I am not the woman you're looking for."

"Interesting," said Mr Esposito, adept at turning disadvantages into advantages. "Very fine. You must know, then, where our Emma Hopkins is currently located, yes?" stated Mr Esposito. "So you may, in fact, be of some assistance to us after all."

Mikey took this statement as a positive one, and shuffled forward, keen to yet receive the praise he'd been hoping for.

"Let me go! This instant!" insisted Abby defiantly. All that was missing from the cliché was a stomp of her shoe and the waving of a fist.

"Or what?" asked Mr Swan, amused, and tilting his head quizzically.

Abby thought for a moment, gathering herself together, and formulating a reply.

"Because, you bloody wazzock, right now, one of the most talented, brilliant investigators I've ever worked with is busting down doors and using his extensive network on this island to find out where I am. He'll already have picked up the trail, and trust me, wherever you go you better have one eye over your shoulder because he's going to snap your neck like a twig! When he catches up with you, you'll rue the day you ever set foot on the Isle of Man!"

$$\mathcal{P}\,\mathsf{Q}$$

"Sam, will you stop sobbing? That's not going to help anyone, now is it?" Emma told Sam as if admonishing a small child, though not without sympathy.

"I'm not crying," insisted Sam, unconvincingly. "I've got something in my eye, is all," he said, wiping the moisture from his cheek, before abruptly abandoning all pretence. *"How could I let them take my Abby??"* he wailed.

Emma moved to him. "Allow me," she said, using a damp tea towel to wipe away the dried blood from his cheek. "You have quite a nasty gash here. It may require some stitches. Have you injured your lower back?" she asked, in reference to Sam rubbing his rump. "Have you whacked your coccyx?"

"What? No!" Sam replied, horrified. "Nothing like that!" he said, misunderstanding. "No," said Sam. "It's these bloody shorts, they've nearly cut me in two."

"So what do we do now?" Emma asked.

"Well, I can promise you they're going straight in the bin as soon as I can get my jeans to change into," replied Sam.

"I'm not talking about your shorts!" Emma responded. "For god's sake, I mean about this current situation. Your friend has been taken, and I cannot stay in this place. They're going to find me in no time if they've got her."

"They'll hurt her?" whimpered Sam.

Emma nodded her head. "If Mr Esposito thinks she knows where I am, then, yes, she's in real danger. As *we* are, also."

"This is pants," said Sam. "I can't just sit here. I'm going to phone the police."

"You can't," Emma reproved. "They've got my sister, remember, and now they've also got your friend. If you go to the police, they wouldn't think twice about killing them. Trust me, I know."

"And you know what *I* know?" said Sam, suddenly angry, throwing the towel on the floor. "All this mess has happened since you came on the bloody scene!"

"It's not been a bundle of joy for me either!" Emma shouted. "Don't forget, thanks to you, I've now got not one but *two* crazed psychopaths trying to hunt me down and kill me!"

Sam bowed his head. "Oh, yeah. About that," he said in a more conciliatory fashion. "I forgot to tell you, I may have misled you — by accident! — about the whole Mr Justus thing."

Emma looked at him hard. "Misled me, how?" she demanded.

"Well... on reflection, I gave him the correct painting, I think. So, technically, it's just the one. Psychopath, that is. Just one, not two. So he — Mr Justus — should be happy?"

Emma's expression softened somewhat. "Well, that's actually good news, I suppose. But it's still like waiting to be eaten by one lion instead of two."

"Would Mr Justus know where Mr Esposito has taken Abby?" Sam was clutching at straws.

"What? No, of course not," Emma replied. "Mr Justus has never met him and probably doesn't even know he exists. I doubt their paths have ever crossed. I'm the only one that's ever met him and all the others who've been ripped off — been involved in every fraudulent transaction — which is one of the reasons my life is expendable in this whole mess. There are numerous people involved in these transactions, but with me being the public face — the man in the middle, if you will — I'm the one who has sufficient knowledge to bring the whole debacle crashing down. This is why Mr Esposito knows that I'm his Achilles heel — the one who knows every aspect of the size and scale of his forgeries. This is why, if he does find me, I will be dead once my usefulness to him had ended."

Sam walked solemnly towards the narrow window, his silhouette filling the ageing wooden frame as he looked at the sun glistening off the water at the nearby Laxey Bay. He could sense Emma's eyes were trained on him about the same time as he felt a gentle breeze caressing his right bum cheek.

"Have my shorts ridden up again?" he asked without looking.

"Yes. Yes they have," replied Emma, with a tone suggesting that this was not a sight she wished very much to see.

Sam gripped the fabric in frustration and yanked it out of its darkened recess, while scooping up his phone (which had been retrieved from the boot of the car) with his free hand.

"You're not phoning the police, are you?? They'll kill my sister and your friend!" said Emma with a fair bit of urgency.

"No," Sam assured her. "But we can't just sit with our thumbs up our arse waiting for them to find us! No, I'm going to do something about this, and the only people that can help us — that I know we can trust — are those two fellows from the FBI."

Chapter Eleven
The Humboldt Penguin

Two young children moved at pace, their heads buried in a folded glossy brochure that they'd opened like an accordion. They giggled with excitement as they ran up the gravel path and pressed their faces up against the glass screen. Their red rain macs and yellow Wellington boots appeared over-cautious on a day where the sun hung high in the sky.

They shuffled sideways to maximise their view while continuing to chatter incessantly. The boy on the right hit his young female companion on the head with the brochure, and began to turn in order to make good his escape. He progressed very little beyond the twisting of his torso, however, before smashing into something which sent him flying backwards. But, before the *boo-hoos* arrived, a hand reached down.

The small boy's gaze progressed northward, slowly, as the little girl took shelter behind him (which was no mean feat as the boy was sat flat on his arse). The boy's smooth, pristine face tilted up, and eventually its eyes came to rest on another face, far above, that looked like it'd seen rather more wear and suffered far more abuse. As such, it was not what anyone might ever mistake for a pretty face. Yet it was not an entirely unkind face.

The boy accepted the hand on offer, and regained his feet. Even after getting his sea legs back, though, there was still a great disparity in height between them — and there was something about the man's face that the boy couldn't quite make sense of. He stood on his toes to gain an even better view, mouth agape. "What happened to your nose, mister?" he asked, finally.

A seasoned, weathered face looked down. It looked as if it might unleash a furious storm at any moment. The boy, even up on his toes, at full height, was still pitifully small against the behemoth before him. He didn't stand a chance.

The boy suddenly regretted his cheek, and he settled back down on the soles his feet, pressing them against the gravel and bracing himself for the sort of impending disaster he felt certain was, well, impending.

The man's face broke into a gentle smile. It was the kind of face that wasn't accustomed to smiling — at least not for a very long time — but wanted very much to do so. As the lips parted, the absence of several teeth came into relief. They were victims, these lost teeth, in a battle that both raged and never ended.

"Joey. At'cher service," the man said. "And what about my nose?" he asked, smiling broadly.

The boy started to laugh. He was relaxed now. The man may have been a beast, after all, but was one that could obviously be reasoned with.

The girl leaned forward and whispered to the boy.

"My sister said you look like the Hulk," said the boy, before turning and listening to further instruction. "But not green though she said she could paint you green if you wanted? you've got a funny accent," he said, without taking a breath.

Joey laughed. It was a deep, fathomless rumble, and seemed to be of the type mostly out of range of human auditory senses. It was a laugh that was felt more than it was heard.

A frame bolt from the enclosure's glass screen fell to the ground. It made a *scutch* noise as it hit the gravel. It had apparently vibrated loose and worked its way out from its mooring.

"You two are quite the pair," said Joey amiably. "What are you here for, anyway? What's your mission?"

"Mission?" the boy replied, tilting his head inquisitively.

"Sure," Joey answered. "Everybody's got a mission they're on."

"We came to see the penguins," the boy said, pleased with himself, certain he'd got the answer correct.

"I'll give you five bucks if you can tell me what type of penguins they are," Joey offered.

"What's a buck?" asked the little girl, still retaining her position of cover behind her brother.

"A buck. A dollar," Joey stated. "Oh, wait," he added, catching up. "I meant to say pounds. That's what they're called here, right? Okay, I'll give you five pounds if you can tell me what type of penguins they are."

The little girl was on tiptoe now, and she jumped on the spot with her hand raised to the sky like she'd been stretched out on a medieval rack. "Me!" she said, dancing in place excitedly. "Me, me!"

Joey smiled, putting one finger to his lips thoughtfully, while the index finger of his other hand bobbed along, counting invisible heads in consideration to call upon. "Anybody?" he asked. "Anybody know the answer? Anyone at all?"

"Me! Me! Me!" the little girl said, squirming. Her high-pitched voice was like a ship's whistle as she shouted in short, tight bursts.

"Ah!" Joey said eventually, as if noticing her for the very first time. "You, there! Behind the boy! Would you like to have a guess?"

"Me, me!" she repeated.

"Alright, then," said Joey, finally putting the poor girl out of her misery. "What are they, young miss?"

She slowly returned her feet completely flat to the earth, and she looked at her brother smugly. Because he wasn't the only one who knew things. She knew things, too. Lots of things.

"*Those* penguins," she said with an air of authority. "Those penguins there. Just there. I can tell you for a fact, because I know these things, of course. These types of penguins, as it happens…"

Now it was the girl's turn, it seemed, to keep Joey in suspense. "Yes?" Joey prompted encouragingly.

"Are-black-and-white-ones!" she shot out, rapid-fire.

Joey didn't want to dampen the enthusiasm shown radiating up to him from the girl's beaming face. He took a five-pound note and, as agreed, handed it over to her — as, technically, she was correct.

"You're absolutely right. They are indeed of the black-and-white variety," said Joey, although the girl was now mesmerised by the five-pound note and paying him no mind. "They're also called Humboldt penguins," he continued professorially, and repeated the name for effect. "Humboldt."

"Bless you!" countered the little boy, laughing at the sound of the funny name.

The lesson was then interrupted, unexpectedly.

"Wait there!" shouted a woman with rosy cheeks trying desperately to keep control of a toddler who was using the restraints to take his mother for a ride (it being unclear who was, in fact, in control of who). She brought her child to a halt in front of Joey like a champion jockey. She looked at the children, to Joey, and then back to the children.

"I've been looking for you two everywhere," she said in between catching her breath. "You mustn't run off like that, I've told you a thousand times." The distressed mother's eyes kept flicking toward Joey and it made him uncomfortable.

Joey offered a smile. "It's my fault ma'am. We were playing a game about the penguins and—"

"Where did you get that money?" asked the mother suddenly, snatching it from her daughter's hand. "Is this yours?" she said accusingly, turning to Joey.

"No. Well, yes, in a way. But—" Joey responded, before being interrupted once again.

"Here," she said, thrusting the note towards him. "Do you work here?" she said, eyes narrow, her manner abrupt.

"What? No," Joey replied, getting a little intimidated by a woman easily less than half his size.

"What do you do here, then?" she asked, continuing the interrogation.

Joey laughed awkwardly. He wondered if she could see the bulge under his jacket, and he played his hand over the buttons, making sure they were fastened, putting himself together. "Well, I suppose I'm just here to help out, I guess you could say."

"Right," was the woman's terse reply. "Well. I'm sorry my children have bothered you," she said, still eying him with suspicion. "Here," she said, holding the five-pound note out again. "Your money."

"No, no, I insist," said Joey, holding the palms of his hands against his chest. "The little girl earned it. She was very good."

Of course this only served to heighten the woman's apprehension, and her eyes, already narrowed, became even narrower.

"Aw, heck, that didn't come out right," Joey appealed. "I meant…"

It was no use. The woman kept hold of the toddler and herded the other two up like a sheepdog. "Move," she said to them through gritted teeth.

The little girl turned to smile at Joey. She was able to offer the hint of a wave before her mum tugged sharply on her other arm, effectively flattening out the wave opposite.

"Don't look at the bad man, Hayley. He looks like he's just been released from prison," said the mum, escorting her brood to safety, and that was the end of it.

The five-pound note was left on the gravel path, its promise abandoned.

Joey had half-raised his hand to return the little girl's wave, and it had remained frozen there when the mother's words hit him — with more force than he'd ever been struck, in any fight, ever. He stood in front of the penguin enclosure and slowly retracted his extended fingers, closing them, until they formed a fist.

He was snapped back to the present when the phone in his pocket started to vibrate. His ringtone was a horse's whinny and the clattering of hooves.

But his phone was on silent now, and, feeling the vibration, he pulled it from his pocket.

Joey wasn't in the mood for pleasantries. "Yes," he barked down the phone. He listened, vacantly. "Yes, yes," he added, bobbing his head, which caused the ripples in his neck to wobble. The phone was almost lost against the backdrop of his enormous head. "The boss asked me to pick a few things up for him," continued Joey impatiently. "Yes. Right. Uh-huh." And then, "Where am I now?" he replied, echoing the caller's question.

Joey stood and twirled, like Julie Andrews on a tranquil meadow — as he basked in the glory of his current location.

"I'm..." he hesitated. "I've dropped by the gym to catch up on some bench presses, what's it to ya?"

The caller must have wanted him somewhere, but Joey's expression clearly said he wanted to be elsewhere. "The boss has got a special job for me. Is that right," he said, rolling his eyes, enthusiasm waning by the second. "Bring a shovel?" he said. "What the flippin' heck am I now, Mikey? The gardener?"

He walked away from the penguin enclosure, in no hurry to leave, just as another young family was gathering there. He lowered the phone for a moment before reinstating back against his cauliflower ear. *Where am I going to get a bag of lime?* "he shouted, before lowering his voice for the benefit of the concerned-looking family nearby.

"Does that even work, anyway?" he said in a hushed voice. "We'd be better hiring a boat and weighing them down with concrete boots? Look, I need to go, I'll be back at the house in about an hour or so. No, I won't forget the shovel, I'm not stupid," he said.

There was a pause. And, then, "What? No, I don't have your... Why would I have your...? Mikey, look, a man does not touch another man's weapon. It's just not done. It's a violation of... okay... okay... right. Exactly. Yeah, I'll see you in about an hour or so."

Joey pressed his hand to his forehead. "Eff this," he said. "Eff this," he said, once again. The appearance of a wandering flamingo had the same effect on Joey as marijuana did on a dopehead. He could feel the stress oozing out of his body, just then, but only momentarily, until the phone rumbled in his pocket once again.

There was no peace for Joey. He ignored it. He doubled back on the path he walked up earlier, passing the penguins on the way. He grimaced for a moment as something poking up caught him sharply in the ribs. He shuffled with his belt and his crotch to adjust it. An undernourished chap, wearing a yellow high-viz jacket and pushing a wheelbarrow, approached Joey at speed as soon as he observed him seemingly getting too friendly with himself in front of the penguin enclosure — but soon stopped when the scale of Joey became all too apparent.

Joey continued to struggle. It wouldn't fit back where it should be, and he had grown tired of hiding it anyway. It was time.

"Bastard," he said, and he began undoing his jacket, one button at a time, in a deliberate fashion — causing the scrawny park keeper to retreat further back.

Joey took the cattle prod, unsheathing it from its anchor, breathing in so as to release it from the grip of his trouser belt, and held it aloft like Excalibur.

The prod — his partner's weapon of choice — had served them well on a number of occasions, despite Joey's own distaste for it. Today he looked at it with utter contempt. Not just because it'd chaffed his gentle areas through the constant rubbing while concealed — How did Mikey ever tolerate it? Maybe, to him, this was part of its charm? — but because it was the very symbol of a life from which he wanted out.

He held the prod in his right hand, took one final look at it, and then lobbed it over the glass barrier like a hand grenade into the foot-deep water of the penguin enclosure.

It was liberating, but even he knew that you didn't just walk out like you would in an office job. It wasn't that simple, unfortunately. And if he was told to complete a job, he had to, without any hesitation, complete the job. Otherwise, it would be he who'd find himself on the receiving end.

Joey stomped toward the park keeper. "Can I buy that off you?" he said in reference to the shovel poking out of the man's wheelbarrow.

"Take it!" came the reply, as the shovel was handed over with shaking hands. "It's my spare one anyway. I don't need it," the man offered, nervously.

"You wouldn't happen to have any lime in there by any chance, would you?" pressed Joey, peering into the mobile workplace.

"Sorry," the man replied weakly, turning even paler.

"Don't worry about," Joey replied. "I'll manage." And he turned to leave.

Joey smiled to himself as the symbol of a world he no longer wanted floated gently around the pool. He placed the discarded five-pound note into the collection tin in the reception area on the way out.

Unfortunately, for a compassionate animal lover, Joey's act of defiance had left an undesired effect. Several penguins had apparently assumed the foreign object in their pool to be some formerly unseen fishy treat. The sound of a young girl screaming carried on the wind as she watched in horror the tableau before her. The Humboldt penguins, as it turned out, lay floating on their back, with their muscles convulsing, one after another, as they each, in turn, attempted to consume the queerly-shaped fish.

But the penguins weren't dead. At least, not yet. The voltage in the pool caused their flippers to flap like a hummingbird's wings, and it was entirely possible that the Isle of Man Wildlife Park would be witness to the first flight of a flightless bird. One last hurrah, perhaps, until it all came crashing down.

Joey remained blissfully unaware of any of this, as he pulled out of the carpark with a somewhat contented look upon his face.

Chapter Twelve
The Family Business

"So, you're in the family business also?" asked Abby with a sneer.

"What?" snapped Madeline in response.

"The forgery business. Does your creative talent extend to reproductive artworks?"

Madeline rolled her eyes. "Oh, yes, that's very clever," she said. She paced the impressively polished floor — the sort of floor a small boy's knees would be attracted to, like a magnet — as she fidgeted with one of the white, wooden sash windows which flooded the room with glorious sunshine.

Of course the glorious sunshine was of no advantage to them, being, as they were, held against their will inside the room.

"It's no use," said Abby. "I've tried them all. They're all locked. All sealed up as tight as a duck's arse."

"There must be some way out of here," Madeline responded. "What about the fireplace?"

"What *about* the fireplace?" said Abby. "Do I look like Santa Claus?"

"You're not very jolly, that's for sure," Madeline remarked.

"I am so! I'm perfectly bloody jolly given the right circumstance! But this is not it!" insisted Abby. "And how are either of us meant to get up that chimney, besides?"

Madeline's cheeks flushed. "At least I'm trying to come up with a plan!" she said, throwing a cautious glance to the shaven-headed thug in an ill-fitting suit, sat on a wooden chair, in front of the only door. The man sneered over the top of his newspaper and chuckled at the dilemma faced by his two charges.

"Is the newspaper for looks, then?" Abby called over in frustration. "As I'm sure an ape like you would be more suited to a paint-by-numbers book. If there are any tricky words in that paper you can't work out, be sure to shout, and we'll draw you a pretty picture!"

The shaven ape did not reply. He was used to these sorts of remonstrations, and was immune to their effect.

Madeline chuckled. "No, I'm not, by the way."

"Not what?" replied Abby, performing a series of stretching exercises.

Madeline mirrored her stretching, not only to relieve the tedium but because they'd been stuck in the same room for hours. The man, once again, peered over his newspaper at the ladies exercising, although with a modicum of discretion.

"You asked if I was in the family business. I'm not. My sister inherited the artistic flair. I'm a vet."

When she heard this, Abby's demeanour softened. "Ah," she said. "Then I'm sorry for being so curt with you. I just assumed, well... you know."

Madeline jogged leisurely, on the spot. "It's fine. I didn't even know about my sister's... alter-ego... until a man appeared in my surgery and insisted I come to his car to look at his injured dog. Next thing I know, I'm on a private jet surrounded by the cast of *The Sopranos*."

"How was the dog?" asked the concerned-looking henchman.

"What?" asked Madeline.

"The dog," he repeated, lowering his paper. "Was it okay?"

Madeline looked at Abby and then back to the seated brute. She sensed a glimmer of compassion there that she thought might prove useful. "He was fine," she said softly. "Just fine." She used the interaction as an invitation for further conversation.

"So," said Madeline, moving closer to him. She pushed her elbows into her sides in an attempt to make her womanly charms appear rather more pert. "What's your name, big fella?" she asked.

"Harry," the big fella replied in a barely-audible Southern American drawl. He added an extra syllable to the word, as Southerners often did. He remained seated, staring directly at Madeline's chest, mesmerised, like a charmed snake.

Madeline did little to avert his gaze. "You must work out," she said, sounding like a ten-dollar hooker. "To get such an impressive physique, I mean."

"I guess," Harry with-the-extra-syllable said, eyes fixed.

Abby smirked as Harry lowered the newspaper further, down to his crotch, as if it were now serving a purpose not originally intended.

"Don't worry, Harry. I'm a lot friendlier than the other one over there," Madeline said, nodding over to Abby. "A girl's got to know how to make the best of a situation, doesn't she?" she purred.

Harry coughed, as if trying to snap himself out of a trance. "Back off," he ordered sternly, surly henchman persona resumed. "I know what you're doing."

"That's because you're an intelligent man," said Madeline, piling on the flattery, using every weapon at her disposal.

"Stop it," said Harry, getting flustered. "And get back over there," he said, pointing. "I really mean it!"

"Fine. Be that way!" Madeline returned, and she walked back over to Abby. The pair of them continued to size up their surroundings, but the only viable exit remained covered by a twenty-stone thug.

"How long are we going to be held?" demanded Abby impertinently. There was no reply, so she tried again. "I *said*, when are we going to be let go?"

Harry's excessive blood flow seemed to have returned to normal, allowing him to regain some focus. "You honestly think I've got my finger on the pulse of this operation?" he said with a gruff belly laugh. "I've been following orders, sitting in a practically-empty room watching you two for the last hour. Does that sound to you like a man who's been sitting included around a boardroom table or something, deciding when to let you two free?" To the frustration of Abby and Madeline, the belly laugh continued.

Madeline scoured the room. "Why don't we hit him with our chair?" whispered Madeline, in the absence of any other identifiable weapon.

"And then what?" said Abby. "Besides, if we hit him with a chair it'd just bounce off him. Look at the size of him! He's built like a brick porta-loo. Don't think I'm raining on your ideas, but if by some miracle we managed to knock him out, there are several more just like him on the other side of that door," she said, motioning.

It was deathly still apart from the periodic noise of Harry turning pages. The silence was deafening. Abby had never been good with bodily noises and the sound of Harry's nose whistling each time he breathed was boring into her skull, like a trepanning drill.

"I've got to get out of here," she said through gritted teeth. Abby took a deep breath to compose herself and watched out over the perfectly manicured gardens. Under different circumstances, she could see herself sat under the distant oak tree on a picnic blanket with a glass of something cold, having her feet rubbed by an attractive man in a nice suit as she absorbed the surroundings.

The momentary daydream dalliance was shattered by the return of the melodic nose whistling in regular time, near the door. It had stopped only momentarily, it seemed, only in preparation for the next movement.

Madeline's gaze, however, remained on the oak tree. She squinted to make out details as two men shifted at pace through the gardens. She wouldn't have given them consideration, except these two were different. Rather than merely a set of muscles atop a pair of legs, these two had a sleek elegance about them.

She stood, under the guise of continuing the stretches Abby had initiated earlier, and moved closer to the window. She dipped her head and squinted again, trying to focus on them. Madeline pressed one hand to her forehead and the other rested on her hip and tried to make herself visible by performing a series of sporadic hip thrusts that gave the impression she was having some sort of episode.

"She alright?" asked Harry, with little genuine concern.

Abby shrugged her shoulders and moved to join her by the window. "What are you doing?" she asked. "You look like my dad trying to dance at a wedding."

"Down there," said Madeline, discreetly nodding.

Abby leaned forward, confused. "What?" she whispered.

"Those two men," Madeline replied, "I don't know what's going on, but they're different from the rest. Something's happening. Whether it's a good or bad thing, I don't know."

Abby looked hard. "Holy smokes," she said after a moment. "I recognise those two men from a website!"

"Oh... kay... Well, that was certainly unexpected. Whatever floats your boat, I suppose," Madeline replied, backing slowly away from Abby and returning to her seat.

"No," said Abby, reaching out for Madeline's arm and tugging on her sleeve. "You don't understand. Those two men came to see my friend, Sam. He showed me their pictures on their website."

Madeline was still wary, but she was listening.

"Madeline," said Abby. "Those two men are from the *FBI.*"

"Oh... kay..." Madeline said again. "And I think I see Spider-Man crawling up the wall to rescue us...?"

Abby moved closer. "I'm being completely serious. And I'm not crazy! They're FBI."

Before Abby could elaborate further, a key turning in the door caused Harry to jump to his feet.

"Boss wants them two," said yet another meathead, another in a seemingly endless conveyor-belt supply of hired thugs. "Make it snappy."

"Snappy is the only way I make it," Harry assured his brother-in-arms.

Apparently satisfied with this response, the other brute returned from whence he came.

Abby's mouth went dry as Harry advanced menacingly towards them. For Harry's part, advancing menacingly was something he'd perfected to an art. There were few things he did exceptionally well, but this was certainly one of those things.

"What are you going to do with us?" Abby demanded, defiantly, putting on a brave face.

But Harry with-the-extra-syllable did not respond. He was too busy doing what he did well. He was not finished with the menacing advancement. Not quite yet, at least. It was his favourite part of the job, and he didn't want it to end too quickly.

Abby's heart raced, but the adrenaline rush also ensured that she was not entirely without a certain kind of courage. She wasn't going without a fight. And, once within range, she took the opportunity to kick Harry forcefully in the shin.

For a man of his bulk, he screamed like a young girl as he raised his right leg, rubbing it frantically. He hopped on one foot, and, then, every time he landed, the thud caused the expensive-looking light fittings overhead to swing gently.

Abby snatched up the newspaper and rolled it tightly before using it to poke Harry in the eye. He barked in pain, shifting his soothing hands between his two injuries.

"That's dirty pool!" he wailed, before the tears from the jab to his eye blinded him. "You're not supposed to do that!"

Abby turned to grab Madeline, but Madeline was not without her own devices and had taken up the chair and swung it full force against Harry's standing leg. Poor bloke didn't have a chance. His spare leg was swept from beneath him and he fell to the floor like a sack of potatoes. A very large sack of potatoes.

"Let's go," said Madeline, holding the broken remnants of the chair in her hand as Harry whimpered on the floor. He was in no condition to give chase.

"Which way?" said Abby.

"I don't know," replied Madeline. "It all looks the same. But we need to do something, anything, since it probably won't take Harry long to recover."

Abby frantically tried a hall window, but it wouldn't budge. "If the FBI are about to come smashing their way in, bearing in mind who they're here to arrest, we need to make sure we're not caught in the crossfire. We can't go that way," she said, pointing to the rear of the corridor. "That's where I was brought in."

They moved through the generous corridor with stealth, cautious about making noise on the wooden floor.

"Which one?" said Madeline, when they'd come to two identical-looking doors.

Abby moved close, pressing her ear in turn against each surface.

"I can't hear voices behind either of them," she said. Presented with a 50/50 proposition, she offered, "Let's try this one?" She said this with her ear still very much attached to the door. "But don't make a sound," she admonished.

Unbeknownst to Abby, Madeline had already reached behind her and pressed down on the silver door handle. With Abby's weight still resting against the door, it nearly came off its hinges as it flew open and smashed against the wall. Abby staggered forward but the momentum of her body moved quicker than her legs, which struggled to keep up, and it was a certainty which would win the race. Abby's face planted the floor as she collapsed, unceremoniously, in a heap.

"What happened to don't make a sound?" whispered Madeline.

Abby groaned as she tried to right herself. Her knickers were on display to the world, so with a quick adjustment, she pulled herself up with the assistance of an intricately-carved wooden table. The unexpected motion caused the monumental vase which rested on top of it to stagger like a drunken sailor. It was the size of a small child and quivered precariously. Abby and Madeline both lurched forward and grabbed one of the delicate handles, precluding it from certain demise.

Madeline let go, allowing Abby to place it carefully back on the table, but, before she could do so, Harry's considerable frame came hopping through the door, with a trickle of blood running down his chin.

Harry may not have been the brightest star at the rodeo, but as soon as he saw the vase in Abby's hand he knew what was coming.

He went crashing to the floor once again, with remnants of antique vase now embedded in his forehead.

Abby stood holding the vase handle — all that remained after the impact. "Harry's really not having a good day," she said, tossing it to the floor beside him. "I very nearly feel sorry for him." She said, ushering Madeline through yet another stately room.

"This place is a hellish maze," said Madeline.

"No, that's over there," said Abby pointing to a maze, outside, in the garden.

She could sense that Madeline had fallen behind. "Hurry up," she said with urgency. There was no response, so she turned instinctively. The man who'd given Harry his instructions earlier now stood to the side of Madeline with a gun held against her temple.

"Off somewhere, were we, ladies?" he chuckled as he motioned with the gun for Abby to move forward whilst keeping a firm grip on Madeline.

They retraced their steps.

"The boss is going to be very upset when he sees this," the man with the gun said, once they'd come upon Harry.

"Oh, he'll be fine," said Abby. "Right as rain soon enough."

"I meant about the vase," the man said, stepping over Harry without concern.

"Bloody hell, you henchmen need to learn some compassion," said Abby.

"It was you who put him on the floor," scoffed the henchman.

"Yes, but still, he's still one of your work colleagues," Abby admonished. "It's sort of sad that I'm more concerned about him than you are. I'll bet your work Christmas parties are a right laugh," she said, with no intent to hide the sarcasm.

"Holiday party. They're called holiday parties now," the brute said matter-of-factly. "To be more inclusive."

They were escorted into a formal dining room where Mr Esposito sat in isolation, at the top of a dining table that warranted a state banquet. He looked both somewhat surprised to them and a touch annoyed that his meal had been interrupted.

This was not entirely lost on the brute. "Boss," he said, his voice betraying his unease. "I caught these two trying to make a break for it."

Mr Esposito lowered his fork. "Is that so, ladies?" he said. "Is my hospitality not to your liking?" he asked, with what sounded very much like sincerity. He pushed his chair back and wiped his mouth with a crisp white napkin. "Well. What to do with you two," he said, walking towards them now.

He had an air of something about him. A style and elegance, which, if he weren't a crime boss, could easily come across as charming.

The fight had left Abby, fully aware of what this man could do — or, at least, have performed on his behalf — with a snap of his fingers.

"Let us go," Abby pleaded pathetically. "Please. We've done nothing wrong," she said. "She didn't even know what her sister was up to," she added, looking to Madeline.

Madeline said nothing. She knew it was useless to plead.

Mr Esposito gave a wry smile and returned to his seat. "Soon," was all he said, picking his fork up and setting upon his meal once again.

Abby caught a flicker of movement through a glass door in the far corner of the room. She held her breath when she caught a glance of the same two men from the garden. She shot a discreet glance to Madeline, who gave a quick, knowing nod in return. The two men were running in their direction, towards the door. Mr Esposito, meanwhile, was focused entirely on his meal.

Abby recoiled slightly. After all, their minder was in possession of a gun.

As the door suddenly opened, the men from the FBI burst into the room, weapons drawn.

"Freeze! FBI!" one of the agents shouted, as this is what one might ordinarily be expected to say under such circumstances.

Abby took this as her lead and clenched her fist and swung it like a wrecking ball, catching her captor firmly in his wrecking balls.

He howled when the pain in his groin reached his brain (which, despite the lengthy trip, was quite fast in this instance).

Mr Esposito, for his part, set his cutlery on the table, placing it carefully onto a cloth napkin. Despite the care in which he did this, however, he performed this action with haste.

Mr Esposito was unaccustomed to finding himself at a disadvantage. "Gentlemen…" he began hesitantly.

"FBI!" shouted the shouting man, once again. "You bunch of thieving bastards are coming with us!"

Mr Esposito, after appraising the situation, regained his composure more rapidly than one might expect. He gave the two men a look that would freeze molten lava.

"Think very carefully about your course of action here, gentlemen. I can promise you that continuing on in this fashion will not be beneficial to your career progression. Or, for that matter, your overall health."

The two men looked like naughty boys who'd been caught stealing conkers. They lowered their weapons as well as their heads.

"What the heck are you two doing??" shouted Abby.

The first FBI man, the shouting one, placed his weapon back inside his jacket. "Sorry, boss. But, we just, you know, got into character," he said. "Didn't we?" he added, hoping his mate would back him up.

"Yes, boss," the other FBI man replied weakly, without looking up. "I think… I think it's the outfits that does it," he offered.

"It's definitely the outfits," the first agreed, eager to place blame. "These black suits, they have an effect on you. You can't—"

"These damn black suits," the second cut in.

"Yeah," said the first, as if this were all the justification needed to explain their actions away.

Abby looked at Madeline. *"What the…?"* she mouthed.

Mr Esposito continued his glare and the two men's legs were buckling like that of a punch-drunk boxer. "And where is our Emma Hopkins?" he asked finally, in a tone so casual as to drip menace.

"We don't know yet," replied the braver of the two, the shouter. "But we made contact with some pathetic excuse for a private dick who's been—"

The man stopped in full flow as the phone in his pocket rang. He held his finger aloft to Mr Esposito. "One second, boss. Sorry. There's only one person that knows this number," he said in expectation. He cleared his throat, effecting a change to a more professional persona.

"Yes. This is Agent Weiss," he said in an authoritative manner. He listened to a voice on the other end for several moments before speaking again. "Sam who?" he asked the caller, whilst raising his thumb in delight for the watching audience. His mate was now clinging to his arm like a first date at a horror movie.

"Ah," he said. "Sam. Yes, I remember now. Of course." He bobbed his head as he soaked up every word.

"You're in danger?" he repeated, echoing the caller's words. The FBI man smiled. "Yes, we know you're in danger," he said, throwing Mr Esposito a knowing glance. "We know you're in danger because you're dealing with one of the cleverest, most innovative, and most powerful criminals the world has ever seen," he elaborated, glancing again to his boss for approval, hoping the shameless fawning would please him.

Abby didn't want to believe what she was seeing. She moved a pace forward. *"Sam!"* she screamed. *"They're not what you—!"*

Her minder grabbed her in a headlock and used his spare hand to cover her mouth. Mr Esposito waved his hand like swatting a fly, resulting in Abby being dragged from the room.

The FBI man continued his phone conversation. "That? Oh, that was nothing. The television. A thriller is on. Yes. Now. Now, we can't help you unless we have Emma Hopkins," he said. "Ah-ha," he said. "Ah-ha. Okay. So you're with Emma Hopkins now? Excellent. This is good news. Yes. Of course we'll meet you. When and where?"

He put the phone back in his pocket and delayed his response for maximum impact.

"Well?" asked Mr Esposito.

"Well, boss. We're due to meet Emma Hopkins," he said, looking at his watch. "In about two hours' time. In two hours, Mr Esposito, I've got a funny feeling that the *actual* FBI's star witness is going to be reluctant to do any more talking."

"You said you weren't going to hurt her!" cried Madeline. "Just let her go, with me. We'll disappear. You'll never hear from us again!" she pleaded. Despite her earlier resolution that pleading was, at this point, useless… what else was there to do?

Mr Esposito reflected for a moment before responding. "I said I would not hurt her? Interesting. Because that does not sound like something I would say at all," he said. "No matter. Madeline," he continued. "What I *can* promise is that you, your sister, and our other guest here will most certainly disappear. And I am reasonably confident that I will absolutely never hear from any of you again. What is more, and of equal importance, is that the FBI will also not be hearing from any of you again."

"Now. Where are we meeting them?" he said to 'Agent Weiss.'

"We can handle this for you, boss," Agent Weiss replied.

"I will be accompanying you," Mr Esposito insisted. "I have got entirely too much at stake here. I need to make certain that there are no further distractions. Before we go, please can you make arrangements with your associates Mr Montgomery and Mr Schmidt to take our two guests for a drive on this beautiful island? Somewhere quiet would be preferable," he said. "Somewhere peaceful. For a nice rest."

Mr Esposito smiled sunnily as he walked towards the two men. He put one hand on each of their shoulders. "I never thought I would say this. But, today, the FBI have very much helped me out of a delicate situation. Good work, gentlemen. Good work!"

Chapter Thirteen
Into the Sea

I can't get used to these stupid cars having their steering wheel on the wrong side," said Mikey, also struggling with the gear stick. "And what's with these roads? They're so freaking narrow. And it's like a ghost town. There's nobody round, except for sheep. For pity's sake, I need to get back to the city. To civilisation."

Joey had switched Mikey off, and his head was rested against the passenger-side window. He'd never seen anything quite as beautiful as this island. Wherever he looked, it was green and surrounded on all sides by rolling countryside. *I love this, this feeling of open space,* he thought. *I could live here.*

"You didn't forget the shovel?" asked Mikey, but no response was forthcoming. "Joey," he said, louder, finally getting his partner's attention.

"No, I didn't forget it. I told you, it's in the trunk. Along with a bag of lime," Joey replied, then returned his attention to the scenery flashing by as they sped through yet another winding country lane. "The countryside here is amazing," he said, absently.

"You got that right," said Mikey. He was in agreement as to the many acres of unspoilt land, though for an entirely different reason. "That's the one good thing about this godforsaken backwater. You don't have to drive too far to find somewhere to bury a stiff. Speaking of which…" He looked in the rear-view mirror and chuckled at the two pillowcase-covered figures staring back. "Whaddaya think, ladies?" he said. "You two should be grateful that this car has tinted windows. Otherwise, you'd both be in the trunk with the shovel and the lime."

Frantic muffled noises issued forth from the pillowcases. Neither Abby nor Madeline were able to move, given the generous application of duct tape to their ankles and wrists. Duct tape truly was a miracle invention.

"You definitely brought the shovel?" Mikey asked yet again.

"Why would I forget the shovel?" Joey was letting his irritation show. "What is with you and the shovel?"

"You're going to have to do the digging, Joey," Mikey told him. "Just so you know. Since I've had this sciatica, I'd be in bed for days if I overexert myself."

"What? You think I'm digging two holes myself? That's not happening. Why don't we just throw them in the sea? There was sea near Laxey."

"What's a Laxey? Anyway, there's sea everywhere," replied Mikey.

"Don't be dim," said Joey. "It can't be everywhere."

There was a twinkle in Mikey's eye. He was trying to be clever now. Which was a dangerous thing. "Joey, you do realise what an island is, don't you?"

"Of course I know what an island is," replied Joey flatly.

"Well?" prompted Mikey.

Joey didn't take the bait. He was not in the mood.

Mikey continued to chuckle. He was very pleased with himself. "Joey," he said. "An island is something that's surrounded by water."

There was nothing worse than an idiot who truly believes he is clever. "I'll be throwing *you* in the water,"

Joey assured him. "So, for real, though. Why don't we throw them in the water?"

Mikey thought for a moment. "Well, we haven't got a boat."

"Just throw them in," replied Joey. "The tide will carry them out."

Mikey shook his head. "No, we'd need to take them out, at least a good five-hundred meters. We don't want these two washing back up to shore. At least not until we're thousands of miles away from this godforsaken place."

"You can at least dig one of the ditches, then," Joey responded. "Sciatica or no. Fair is fair."

"Joey, you only need to dig one ditch. One *big* ditch!" Mikey explained. "Besides, we've only got the one shovel, so what am I supposed to do? Dig a hole with my paws, like a dog? See? My logic is perfect. You can't escape it."

"So where am I going to dig this hole?" Joey asked, resigned to his fate. "We can't just keep driving around aimlessly. We should ask for directions."

"Are you freaking' kidding me?" said Mikey. "You want me to pull the car over and ask for directions? To what, exactly? A nice, out-of-the-way place to bury two bodies? Let's ask one of these nice sheep farmers. Maybe they'll even help us dig the hole!"

Joey sank into his seat. "Okay, okay, but we can't just drive around forever. It's not fair on them."

"On them? Them, who?" Mikey replied, perplexed.

"The ladies," Joey answered, pointing a thumb in the direction of the back seat.

"Not fair on them? What does fair have to do with anything? Trust me, this does not have a happy ending for them any way you slice it. So, this driving around is the least of their worries. Over there," said Mikey as he fought with the gear stick, once again. He slowed the car and turned into an even narrower country lane. Judging by the hammering the suspension was currently being subjected to, this was clearly a lane more suitable for agricultural traffic.

"Where are we going?" asked Joey.

"Who's doing the driving?" replied Mikey. "I'm doing the driving," he said, answering his own rhetorical question. He motioned with his head. "Up there," he said. "That old building will be perfect. There are plenty of trees for cover. And, from the looks of the place, nobody is going to bother you while you're digging."

The lane stretched up, following the contour of the steep incline, and was a gateway into the beauty of the isle. From their elevated position, Joey looked down on the glorious valley where the sun radiated off a reservoir in the distance. They turned off the path halfway up the hill, which was fortunate, as the track was all but impassable. Trees peppered the field, with some looking like they'd surveyed this landscape for hundreds of years. Many of them were distorted, as if pushed over — likely from the ardent winds that'd whipped up from the valley and battered them over the decades.

A dilapidated stone building had the privilege of this vista all to itself. Its footprint was small, probably only big enough to provide the former occupant a room to sleep and room to light a fire. The area was exposed, and in a harsh winter this idyllic spot would have been open to the elements. The stone walls were built to last, over two feet thick, and they'd survived longer than the doors and roof which has long since succumbed to the elements.

"I could live here," said Joey, taking a lungful of the bracing Manx air.

"Is there anywhere you wouldn't live, here on this crummy island?" said Mikey.

"I'd live anywhere at all. Anywhere you weren't," Joey replied.

Mikey wasn't listening. "Get the shovel out of the car and we can dig here," he said, kicking out at the softer soil. "You get digging and I'll wait in the car and keep an eye on these two."

Before Joey had time to protest, Mikey was back in the car, seat reclined, shoes kicked off, and his feet planted on the dashboard.

"Douchebag," announced Joey, loud enough to be heard, as he pressed his foot down to remove the first sod from the ground. The earth was pleasingly forgiving. He'd had to complete this task previously — in cold weather — and frost on the ground was a nightmare for causing blisters. It wasn't all bad for Joey, he supposed. He was getting some exercise, and, as far as views from the office went, today's was perfectly palatable.

In no time at all he was knee-high in the ditch, with its former contents sat neatly in a pile and ready to be thrown back in when required. He saw a shimmer of silver and crouched down to pluck an object from the dirt. His heart skipped as his spat on his thumb and used the sizeable digit to wipe away the excess soil. It was a coin.

Joey was delighted, holding the coin up to the sunlight to get a clearer view. He wasn't familiar with the local currency, so he was unable to discern if he'd found a relic, cast aside, hundreds of years ago, or merely some child's pocket money. No matter. Joey placed it in his pocket for later inspection. He looked at his watch and became conscious of how long their guests had been sitting in the back of the car. Joey never liked to keep a lady waiting. It was bad manners.

"Hello, friend," said a perky voice.

Joey nearly had a coronary. He dropped his shovel and jumped out of his expanding hole, like a rat up a drainpipe. He couldn't see anyone. He thought Mikey was messing with him but ruled this out when he could just make out a vague, fleshy outline through the tinted glass. The sound of snoring from the car's front seat confirmed that Mikey was not the owner of the voice.

Joey held his arm aloft and used his hand to deflect the sun from his eyes. He scoured the field once again, but still nothing. It took a moment for his eyes to adjust, but he could just make out a figure — dressed head-to-foot in camouflage — moving toward him. The figure blended perfectly to the backdrop, so the clothing had served its purpose quite successfully.

The figure moved closer and appeared to be brandishing a weapon. Joey placed his hand inside his jacket and prepared to draw his firearm.

"Hello, friend," the voice — now audibly male — called out once again.

Joey was milliseconds away from having to find space to accommodate a third corpse. Whether it was the scenery or the fresh air, Joey was feeling charitable, and he delayed unleashing a volley of lead. Despite this, the sight of the camouflage, eventually — for it was particularly good — filled him with panic. Were the Army onto him? He thought for a second, ticking off various modes of response, and he weighed his options.

As the figure moved from the shadows, it became apparent that the offensive weapon was in actual fact a metal detector, however, and the person wielding it merely a scrawny middle-aged man who looked like he would still live at home with his mother.

The man overexaggerated a wave and gave Joey an overemphasised smile. This man clearly did not realise how close he currently was to death.

"I've not seen you around here before," he said, with a jolly expression. "Are you detecting?" he asked, scanning the ground for machinery.

Joey relaxed a little but remained poised. "Sure," he said slowly, in response to the question. "Detecting."

"You're a little smartly dressed?" the camouflaged detector said in reference to Joey's immaculate black suit and polished shoes that were now partially covered in mud. "My name is George," George said, offering a handshake which Joey grudgingly accepted.

"I like to make an effort," replied Joey. "So, you, uh, you like digging stuff out of the ground, do you?"

"Oh, I love it," George responded, with genuine enthusiasm. "Digging things up is my life!"

"Great!" said Joey, reaching into his pocket. He took out the coin and pressed it under the nose of the quizzical visitor.

"Where did you find this?" George asked, barely able to contain his excitement.

Joey looked at George, then down to the big hole in the ground and then back to George. "I found it in this hole," said Joey.

"You know what you've found?" said George, all but dancing on the spot. "Do you've any idea?"

Joey was not a man who readily displayed emotion, but he was now salivating like Pavlov's dog. "It's valuable, is it?" he asked.

George took one final look. "Nah," he said. "It's from about nineteen-sixty, actually. And dead common."

George started to laugh to an extent that a snot bubble formed and burst over his top lip. "I had you going there, though, didn't I? I had you going good!"

Joey reached back inside his jacket. George was about to be severely pistol-whipped.

"Don't be down in the dumps," continued George. "We have a club. With patches you can sew on. And membership certificates. You should join. Meet the lads! I'll take you out and show you the ropes. You'll be a professional before you know it, you'll see!"

George was like an eager puppy — very difficult, as it turned out, to kill. Joey took a look over his shoulder and could still make out the sleeping form of Mikey.

"George," said Joey. "George, men have died for doing less to me than that. But I like you, George. Now, I'm about to do something to you that, when you wake up, you won't be immediately grateful for. But, trust me, there are currently two outcomes for you. And this one, believe it or not, is the one you want."

George screwed up his eyes, unsure what was going on, and began to laugh, nervously. "What do you mean by..."

Joey jabbed him on the chin. Not full pelt, but sufficient to render him unconscious. Joey was like an anaesthetist; one could very reasonably describe him as a consultant of unconsciousness. Like a consummate professional, he'd calculated the optimum force required but without causing permanent damage.

Joey picked him up like he was carrying his shopping. If Mikey woke up and saw him, George was a dead man, of course. There was nothing for it. And so Joey carried him, very quietly, around the corner of the building and dumped him in a bush that'd thrived in the harsh conditions and would likely continue to thrive. Joey was dejected about the coin, but he smiled as he covered George's feet. Joey had just saved a man's life. It was a first for him, and he found he liked the feel of it very much.

He returned to his shovel and looked at his shoes. "Crap!" he shouted, as he tried to rid himself of the filth, to wipe it away onto the grass. "I'll never get all this off now!"

"Is that all you've done?" shouted Mikey, roused from his slumber, from the comfort of the car.

"What?" asked Joey. "It's done. You need to buy yourself some glasses. Get them two out of the car."

Mikey dragged the women who were, to say the least, reluctant to leave the car — like Mikey, earlier, though for entirely different reasons. He escorted them over to Joey, but, with ankles bound, progress was slow. As they kept tripping over their own feet, Mikey removed the pillowcases to restore their ability to see. The sight of a shovel and a hole, of course, did little to calm Madeline and Abby.

Mikey did nothing to hide his frustration. "What's that?" he said looking at the hole that would, at best, be described as a shallow pit. "A kid with a plastic bucket and spade could've made better progress by now. Seriously, what the—?"

He never got a chance to finish, however, as Dr Joey Schmidt, the anesthesiologist, had not yet clocked off. He walked forward two paces and delivered a right hook that connected with Mikey's chin with medical precision. Mikey Montgomery was unconscious before he crashed to the earth below. Joey clapped the palms of his hands in satisfaction as Mikey dribbled.

Joey moved towards the two women, who recoiled as best they could — which, considering their bindings, wasn't much. Madeline closed her eyes, bracing for the inevitable, as Joey produced a knife, which had been strapped to his ankle, and advanced it in the direction her face.

With the skill of a butcher, the gag around her mouth was cut free, allowing her to take a hungry gulp of air. He continued with similar slashing motions, and both women were, in short order, released from their restraints.

"Are you going to kill us?" asked Abby.

Joey laughed. "I should. But, no. I'm not. I can see you're both desperate to run away. But, honestly, I won't hurt you. If I wanted to, I would've done it by now. If you don't mind waiting for a few minutes, I'll give you a lift to wherever you need to go."

Abby rubbed her wrists, still sore from having been bound. She looked at Madeline for assurance.

"And what about this one?" Madeline asked her captor-turned-saviour, motioning with a nod to the crumpled heap that was Mikey Montgomery. "How are you going to stop him from telling Mr Esposito that you let us go? Are you going to kill him now? Because if you were going to kill him, that wouldn't exactly break my heart."

Madeline massaged her neck, trying to get the kinks out, and then did some twists to loosen up her back. "I might even help," she added.

"Once again, I should. But I won't. Wait here a sec, okay?" Joey said to them.

Joey took the shovel back to the car, opened up the boot, and returned the shovel from whence it came. He removed a tatty-looking brown fabric hold-all. He marched with purpose back over to Mikey and picked up his arm, feeding the hand through the handle, and then placing it carefully back down by his side.

"C'mon," said Joey. "Let's get out of here."

Joey opened the car door, this time like a proper gentleman, and the relief on the women's faces was evident. Joey was half in the car when he stopped.

"One minute," he said, marching back over to the house. He was tempted to give Mikey a kick as he passed him, but continued round the corner, leaving him unmolested.

Madeline and Abby peered out the window, unsure where he'd gone. "Does this man collect bodies?" asked Abby as Joey appeared with the barely-conscious detectorist slung over his shoulder.

"I couldn't leave this guy. Mikey would most probably kill him if he found him," Joey offered by way of explanation.

George lay with his head rested on Madeline's lap. His eyes opened briefly but they soon glazed over and he drifted off, once again, into slumberland. "I shouldn't have eaten that boysenberry pie," he muttered, just before he did.

Joey carefully completed a three-point turn, taking care to avoid the larger rocks, and started back down the narrow lane.

"What about your partner?" asked Madeline, glancing behind them. "You're just going to leave him there?"

Joey shook his head. "Yes and no. See, you guys are going to phone the police when I drop you off. You're going to tell them where he is. And I've got a funny feeling that, today, they're going to find the largest stash of cocaine that's ever been recovered on this island."

"That bag you placed around his arm," Abby said, nodding. "And what then? What about you?" she asked.

Joey paused for a moment before replying.

"Because I've saved your life today, I've put a death sentence on my head. I'm hoping you remember that when you speak with the police. But, while Joey Schmidt still has breath in his lungs, Joey Schmidt is going to get off this island and do something that Joey Schmidt wants to do."

"Speak about yourself in the third person?" Madeline suggested, hazarding a guess.

Abby released a large sigh of relief as she adjusted George's feet. "Shit!" she suddenly shouted.

"Schmidt," Joey corrected her.

She put her hands to her face. "Crap, I forgot about Sam! Joey, do you know what they did with my friend, Sam?"

Joey shrugged. "No idea. But if he's with that artist woman, then I wouldn't bet on his chances of survival."

"*That artist woman* is my sister!" protested Madeline.

Abby reached for her phone, but it wasn't there. Then she remembered it'd been taken from her. "Joey, I need your phone. I have to call him and warn them. Please."

Joey threw his phone into the back seat. Abby was frantic. "What's the password?" she shouted.

"Bambi," Joey replied.

Abby blinked, eyes wide, but didn't question it. She pressed the keys, but her fingers were operating quicker than her brain could process. "Pick up, pick up," she said, finally successful, and with the phone to her ear. "Sam, it's me! Don't meet those two guys, they're not... Oh, hell! Bloody answer machine! Why does he have a bloody phone if he doesn't answer??" she said in desperation.

She held her head in her hands. Every possible eventuality ran through her head. She knew her options were limited. "Joey, you have to take me back to the house in Laxey. That's the only place I can think to go. I'll give you directions, but you need to be quick. If we don't do something, those two fake FBI tosspots are going to kill Sam and Madeline's sister. Joey, you need to step on it!"

"Sure," said Joey, ever the faithful servant. "I'm just going to pull the car over and we can leave George here by the side of the road. He'll be fine, I think. Probably think he's detected an entire car bumper-first or something."

Once they'd pulled over, Joey picked him up once again, and placed him gently against a grass verge, safely away from the edge of the road. "He'll be okay here," said Joey, reassuring himself as much as the others. "Oh," he added, knocking on the car window. "Pass me out his metal detector, will you? I was tempted to steal it, but from now on, Joey's a reformed character."

"Next stop, Laxey," he said, sliding back into the driver's seat, pressing the pedal to the metal, tyres spinning as they found purchase, and leaving a cloud of dirt and gravel in their wake.

Chapter Fourteen
Piss on Your Chips

Joey's abilities at disposing of surplus corpses was bettered only by his skill behind the wheel. Madeline and Abby's knuckles were white as they clung onto the rear grab-handle for fear of being catapulted through the window.

Still...

"You're slowing down, Joey?" said Abby. "Why would you do that, Joey? You need to speed up! Speed up!"

Joey shook his head. "This car isn't much good to you if we've got the police chasing us. Besides that, this car has probably been involved in more murders than Jim Rockford."

"Jim Rockford?" Abby asked, confused.

Madeline was about to translate, but Joey beat her to it. "Miss Marple," he said.

"Oh. I see," replied Abby.

"Yeah. And I could really do without attracting any additional heat. If you catch my drift," Joey responded.

"Catch your...?" But Abby decided it wasn't worth trying to work out. "I'll try Sam's number again," she said. It was evident by the aggressive profanity a moment later, however — of which a drunken sailor would've been proud — that Sam's phone was still going to answer machine.

"What if we're too late?" said Madeline in despair. "What if those two goons got to them first?" The blood drained from her face. "We should phone the police," she said desperately, reaching for the phone.

"And say what, precisely?" Abby replied, putting her hand over Madeline's. "We don't know where they are yet. We also don't know what that psychopath Esposito will do if the police turn up en masse. We've actually got an advantage at the moment."

Madeline was not overly convinced, and her expression did little to hide her feelings.

"Think about it," Abby continued. "Mr Esposito thinks we're both dead, or dying. He doesn't know that Joey has gone rogue on him. We've at least got the element of surprise on them."

"I'm not sure how that's going to help," said Madeline. "I don't mean to piss on your chips. I just don't know how we can do anything. We don't even know where they are."

"Hang on. Did you just say *piss on your chips?*" Abby asked, impressed.

"I pick things up!" Madeline replied. "Anyway, shouldn't we maybe go back to Mr Esposito's house?"

"You'll be going all by your lonesome," said Joey, from the front. "Are we here?" he asked, passing by a huge *WELCOME TO LAXEY* sign.

"Yes," said Abby. "Take the next right. Don't go too quick, it's really steep and there's a narrow bridge on the way down," she told him. "What do we do if Mr Esposito is there?" she asked.

"Leave that to me," said Joey. "He doesn't know I've punched Mikey's lights out. If he or any of his goombahs are in there, I can make something up. Or at least give you two the heads-up you'll need to make yourself scarce."

Abby smiled. "Thank you, Joey. I mean that. Just think, Joey, you're no longer a ruffian. You're technically a retired ruffian," she told him. "Just up that lane on the left," she added, pointing to show the way.

Joey pulled the car up and gestured for the two women to stay in the car. "If I'm not back in two minutes, get running," he said, pulling out his gun.

The holiday cottage was covered on all sides by a rainbow of flowers, and enclosed by a waist-high white picket fence. Joey looked for a discreet point of entry, but for a brute of a man like him discretion would often prove challenging. After discounting any other form of entry, he pushed on the flimsy-looking gate — but it resisted his advances.

Joey looked over his shoulder to make sure he wasn't followed, before stooping over to see how the gate was fastened. There was nothing obvious to be seen, so he tried again, with a little more pressure. But, once again, the little white wooden bastard of a gate wouldn't shift. All hopes of a covert entry were gone when he placed his shovel-like paws on top of the gate, giving a final forceful nudge... with the gate coming clean off in his hands.

"Crap!" he said, flapping his hand to dislodge it. The knuckles on his right hand had slipped between the wooden slats and he now wore the gate on his wrist, like some gaudy oversized wooden bracelet. He placed the gate between his legs and used the resistance to try and break free, but every time he tried to release it, folds of skin on his hand formed and blood was prevented from circulating around his pale-looking digits.

Mr Clover, from Clover's Cottage, was a permanent fixture. Permanent in that he didn't rent out his cottage, rather living in his full-time. The sound of splintering wood had interrupted his garden maintenance (his garden maintenance being a somewhat continuous endeavour). His head appeared, as if floating, from behind his perfectly-manicured privet hedge. He adjusted his glasses, which were as thick as milk bottles, and zoomed in on the hulking figure of Joey presently having some sort of disagreement with his neighbour's fence. "This simply will not do," he said, picking up his trowel and marching with vigour to intercede. "Not if Francis Clover has anything to say about it. No, sir."

Joey, normally keen on remaining aware of his surroundings, was at that moment preoccupied.

"What are you doing, you great lout?" Mr Clover demanded.

Mr Clover continued his advance. As he was an ageing pensioner, however, his 'vigorous march' was in fact a rather protracted shuffle.

Joey was too engaged in his current struggle and began to smack his wooden wrist accessory on the remaining intact segment of fence. He cursed as a trickle of blood ran down his fingers.

"Put that down, this instant!" shouted Mr Clover. He was getting close now. Just a little farther…

Joey became aware of a small yapping sound, and looked over his shoulder to discern the source of the noise and assess its importance.

It was an elderly gentleman, brandishing a trowel, and gesticulating with it in pointed jabs to the air.

"Put that fence down, or you'll get a good thrashing, I can promise you that!" came the final demand from Mr Clover, almost on top of Joey.

Now Mr Clover was a few feet away, however, the sheer scale of Joey seemed to become apparent. Mr Clover adjusted his glasses, once more, as if to confirm that the image his brain was receiving was indeed correct.

"I'm *trying* to put the stupid thing down!" Joey protested. I've *been* trying! But it's stuck!"

Like a scrappy Yorkshire terrier picking a fight with a Rottweiler, there was still some fight left in Mr Clover — though some of the wind had been taken from his sails, and his garden trowel now drooped in his hand. "I've been in the war, you know!" he managed, and gave his trowel a bit of a wave like it was the Union Jack.

Which war Mr Clover had been in was unclear. Judging from his advanced age, it could very well have been any of them. Or all of them.

Blood continued to run down Joey's hand, and, bizarrely, seemed to be acting as a lubricant. Joey could feel it beginning to give way, and took advantage of this by giving it a tremendous tug. Considering the force exerted, when his hand eventually did come free, the result was that it was released with the speed of a champagne cork.

The momentum caused Joey to stagger sideways, and his out-of-control fist continued on its trajectory like a comet — in this instance, Haymaker-Levy. Joey grimaced as it made impact, coming to an abrupt halt on Mr Francis Clover's chin.

"Old-timer? Are you, um… okay?" asked Joey, stood peering down on the unconscious pensioner, though he was afraid he already knew the answer. "Crud," he said, knowing he had to act fast. Joey had been outside the cottage for less than four minutes and had already destroyed the fence and sparked the neighbour clean out. Things were not going according to plan. Granted, there'd been no real plan to speak of. But, still.

"Come on, you're coming with me," he said, picking Mr Clover up and placing him under his arm like a roll of carpet. Joey attempted to rest the gate in its original position, but it simply collapsed to the ground (much like Mr Clover had done).

Joey entered the cottage and placed his unexpected companion in a high-backed armchair located in the hall and looked for any sign of Mr Esposito, or indeed anybody — but the cottage turned out to be empty.

"Joey, are you okay in there?" said a whispered voice from the front garden. Joey jumped with a start.

Abby cautiously poked her head through the doorframe. Her gentle expression was replaced by one of fury. "Bloody hell, Joey!" shouted Abby. "We thought you'd been attacked! You told us to go if you weren't back in two minutes. That was ten minutes ago!"

"You don't follow instructions very well, then, do you?" Joey replied.

Abby was seemingly less nervous in his company by now, judging by the slap she threw in the direction of his right shoulder. "We were worried about you!" she said. She took a deep breath in an attempt to placate her racing heartbeat.

The placating didn't last very long.

"What the...??" she screamed, jumping backwards. "Who the hell is *he?"* she said, pointing to the slumped figure in the armchair.

"I think he lives next door?" replied Joey with a casual shrug, as if this sort of thing happened all the time. "I didn't catch his name."

Abby moved a step closer. "Great," she said. "Do you have a habit of collecting bodies wherever you go? So what's he doing in this chair? Is he dead?" she asked.

"Relaxing, at the moment, I'd say," Joey replied, with another shrug.

Abby could see the man was no threat, primarily by the fact there was no motion save for the river of saliva travelling down the fellow's chin. She placed her fingers against his neck. "He's alive," she announced.

"Great," said Joey, distracted now and not really listening.

Satisfied the shovel wouldn't be required for another corpse, Abby began combing the cottage. It didn't take long as it was tiny. "There's nothing here?" she said after a very short while.

"There's nothing here," Joey confirmed.

Joey opened the fridge door for something to eat, but the shelves were empty. "What about this?" he said, picking up a yellow sticker that appeared to have lost its stick from the front of the fridge door and dropped to the floor. "In your line of work, it might be considered... a clue? Anything of importance there?"

Abby's eyes widened. "Maybe, Joey... maybe," she said, reading the note. "What time is it now?"

"Three p.m.," Joey replied.

"This note says *four p.m. at C O*,'"said Abby, now pacing, and with her right hand placed on her chin. If she had a beard, she would have been stroking it.

The front door crashed open, causing Joey to take an immediate defensive stance and reach for his gun.

Madeline stood in the doorway with a garden fork in hand, like a Roman centurion. "Oh. *Okay,* are we?" she said. "Well that's nice to know. I've only just been sitting in that car *scared senseless,* so don't worry about *me* or anything! Abby, you said to give you *three minutes* and it's been *eight.* I've been counting. *Manually.*"

"The two of you are *both* useless at following instructions, then!" advanced Joey.

Madeline held her chest. "I'm glad you're both okay, at least," she said, on the verge of hyperventilating.

"We're just finishing up here," Joey told her. "Have a seat, if you want. We'll be done soon," suggested Joey, knowing she hadn't yet seen the (formerly) trowel-wielding pensioner.

"Thanks," replied Madeline. "Don't mind if I do, actually."

It worked out better than Joey had even hoped, as she eased her bum into the seat without even looking down behind her first. She encountered an obstacle, of course — in the person of Francis Clover — but her focus remained on her surroundings and not on the seat beneath her. And so she wriggled her cheeks on the lumpy chair, seeking comfort, like a cat circulating a sofa before finding an agreeable spot.

Madeline froze, and the blood drained from her face as a pair of bony hands gripped her by the waist. She twisted her head, and, witnessing in true horror-film fashion the spectre of an old man emerging from the seat cushions, wailed like a banshee.

"Oh, I say," said Mr Clover. "This is a wonderful turn of events." He hadn't expected to find an attractive female gyrating on his lap, one would imagine. "I could quite get used to this."

"You filthy thing!" shouted Madeline, as she realised this was in fact an actual person and not a phantasm, and, in response, managed to skillfully jump, twist, and slap Mr Clover in the face in one fluid movement.

"I was in the war, you know!" protested Mr Clover.

Rather than intervene and bring the affair to an end, Joey stood and laughed a laugh that sounded like it originated from his feet.

"We don't have time for this!" shouted Abby like a schoolmarm. "Madeline, stop getting Mr, em…"

"Francis Clover. At your service," said Francis Clover. "And at *yours*, my dear," he added, in Madeline's direction, with a wink.

"Leave Mr Clover be, and stop getting him overexcited," Abby admonished.

"I've been in the war!" Mr Clover said again, though no one knew quite why.

Madeline, nonplussed, was about to respond but Abby spoke again first.

"We've not got time for shenanigans! We don't have much time to figure out where the others are going to be. If we don't figure out where 'C O' is, and stop them going there, they'll meet those fake FBI knobs and—"

"Get their heads blown clean off," said Joey.

Abby stared at Joey for a moment. "Thanks for that, Joey!" she said, sensing the distress on Madeline's face. She placed a hand on Madeline's shoulder, but knew the aid and comfort it provided was very limited. Abby was all nerves herself.

"Hang on. Where am I?" asked Mr Clover, a bewildered expression over his face. "I thought I was in Heaven, a moment ago, but..."

Abby's compassion was required elsewhere, and she moved over to Mr Clover. "You're just next door, my lovely," she said in a soothing tone. "You must have had a fall. Because my friend," she said, pointing to Joey. "Found you outside and brought you in to make certain there was no permanent damage."

"The war..." he said, his voice trailing off. "I was..." Mr Clover kneaded his forehead. He knew something was amiss, but what it was, precisely, was out of reach. Eventually, he dusted himself down and edged slowly towards the front door whilst keeping a distrustful eye on Joey.

Joey was unaware of Mr Clover's eyes on him. His consideration was elsewhere, instead inspecting something he'd recovered from the darkest recess of the cupboard. "A doughnut!" he said. "Guys, I found a doughnut!

I didn't think you even had doughnuts over here. Just crumpets or something."

"We're not savages," Abby replied in disgust, and then turned her attention back to Mr Clover.

"Should we take you to hospital?" she asked. But, as she moved forward, Mr Clover redoubled his efforts at retreat. Realising her offer of further assistance would be rebuffed, Abby raised her hands to show her attentions were friendly.

"I was in the war," he muttered. "I was in the war. I know things. I know loads of things. They tried to get it out of me, but they couldn't. Not Francis Clover. Nossir."

"Francis," Abby said, gently. "I don't suppose you saw my friends that were staying here, did you? A woman with auburn hair and a baldish man? It's important. They're in trouble. They're in danger."

Mr Clover thought for a moment. "That fence," he said, with a glimmer of recognition. He gave Joey another suspicious glance, but his recollection was still too cloudy to pull it all together. "Someone interfering with the fence. It'll come back to me. It'll come back. I still have my mind. My mind is…"

"It's alright, dear. Take your time," said Abby, soothingly.

"Wait," said Mr Clover. "Hang on. I saw the woman you mentioned. I *did* see that woman. But the bloke she was with wasn't bald. He had dark hair, but it looked like it didn't belong to his head. Terrible hairstyle. Terrible. One of those mop-tops that are fashionable these days, I expect, since those four lads became popular. The Ladybirds. That's them. I remember things. I do. I still have my mind."

"One of Esposito's men must have taken Emma?" said Madeline. *"We're too late?"* she asked, clearly in distress.

"No!" Abby immediately replied excitedly. "Hold on." She turned back to Mr Clover. "Could it have been a wig, Mr Clover?" she asked.

Mr Clover thought for a moment. "Hmm, I suppose it could've been, at that," he replied. "That'd make more sense, now I think on it, since I haven't seen those moptop hairstyles for a few years now."

Abby's face lit up as she placed her hands over Madeleine's shoulders. "That must be Sam!" she said, all but jumping on the spot. "He has this fascination with wigs that he's started to do when going deep undercover," she explained. "Well, he's only done it the one time. But this is the second time."

She returned to Mr Clover once more. "He wasn't wearing ridiculously tight shorts, was he? Oh, never mind. At least we know they're both alive. Mr Clover, just one more thing," she said, doing Miss Marple proud. "Did they give you any clue where they were going?"

"Why would they tell me?" asked Mr Clover. "I look like a nosey neighbour? Oh, wait," he continued, with his memory fog lifting further. "I think I did ask the fella, now you mention it. He said he was taking her to his favourite spot on the isle," he said. "Right, I'm going now," he added abruptly.

He exited the cottage and walked up the garden, one eye over his shoulder. He must have forgotten about the gate, which he attempted to open but encountered only its remnants.

Abby waved and gave a smile. "Thank you, Mr Clover! You've saved lives today!"

"It's what I do," Mr Clover muttered to himself, before disappearing again into his own garden.

"Joey, you broke that gate, you should go and fix it. Also, Joey, I don't think you should eat that doughnut, it's got green bits on it. If you fix the gate, I'll buy you a new one. Maybe a whole bag," she said, tapping him on the back, just as he was about to pop the entire doughnut into his mouth in one go.

"The green bits aren't supposed to be there?" Joey replied. He examined the doughnut, contemplating as to whether he should eat it anyway.

"So where's he taken my sister??" interjected Madeline. "We don't have much time!"

"I know, I know," said Abby, pacing once more.

"Well where is his favourite spot on the island?" pressed Madeline. "If we don't get to them before the fake FBI goons, my sister is as good as dead."

Abby recounted every nonsensical conversation she'd had with Sam. Her brain was at bursting point, because there were a seriously large number of nonsensical conversations to consider. She started to laugh, suddenly, which infuriated Madeline.

"This is serious! Why are you laughing?" said Madeline. "Think!" she demanded.

"I bloody am," said Abby. "But he's been coming to this island since he was a kid. And, also, once you know Sam, he does talk a lot of rubbish. I'm trying to filter out the rubbish, but it's difficult. And also pretty funny."

"Are you totally deranged? Have you also had a blow to the head?" asked Madeline, incredulous.

"Do you know what he does?" asked Abby, wistfully. "On a cold day, if we need to go out in the car, he'll run out and start the engine so the air is warm when I get in. Oh," she continued. "For my birthday, he paid for a full mariachi band to surprise me at work — violins, trumpets, and guitars. The full ensemble. The timing wasn't great as I was in the middle of telling a woman I'd found her dog — well, what was left — when the Mexicans burst in."

Abby sat down. "Oh, god! Sam," she said, as the tears flowed. "I always treat him like he's some sort of idiot, but he cares, I mean he really does."

"I think this doughnut is still good," said Joey to no one in particular.

Madeline slapped her hand on the table, hard. "Snap out of it, woman! Pull yourself together! You having a trip down memory lane isn't going to help him! Is it??"

"I know," moaned Abby. "But he loves everything about this place. It's why he moved over here."

"He must have one *special* place," said Madeline. "Think."

Abby raised her hands aloft as if seeking divine inspiration. "He loves going up Douglas Head. He takes his fish and chips and mushy peas up there and watches the boats come and go. He said it always reminds him of how excited he used to get, as a kid, when the boat finally arrived after the long journey across the Irish Sea."

"I think these green things are supposed to be there," Joey remarked.

"We don't have time for a history lesson!" said Madeline.

"Alright, alright! I'm just trying to work out what 'C O' could mean." Abby placed her head on the table and covered her ears as if drowning out any distraction. Then she lowered both hands and drummed her fingertips on the table, much to the annoyance of Madeline. "It's how I think," Abby told her.

"I definitely think these green things are supposed to—" Joey began.

"I've got it!" screeched Abby, who raised her head like a startled meerkat. "*C O*... must mean *Camera Obscura*. There's one on Douglas Head! Come on, we have to go and warn them!"

"What the hell is a Camera Obscura?" Madeline asked, chasing after Abby.

"Come on, Joey, you're driving! We need your skills!" Abby called after them. "We need to get to Douglas Head *tout de suite* and warn Sam and Emma! And, Joey? Step on it!"

"Coming!" Joey shouted back. And, then, to himself, "This is still good." And he popped the doughnut into his mouth before exiting the cottage and getting underway.

Chapter Fifteen
The Camera Obscura

The Isle of Man is steeped in nostalgia, mementoes from a time when numerous passenger ships struggled to keep pace with the influx of passengers. The island was once littered with Victorian innovations, designed to part eager tourists from their hard-earned wages.

One such curiosity was the Great Union Camera Obscura, located in an enviable position on Douglas Head, perfectly positioned, ironically, to keep a watchful eye on those ferries that'd completed the journey across the Irish Sea. It was a fairly intimate, wooden structure — like a miniature circus tent — that contained eleven camera lenses, giving its inquisitive patrons a voyeuristic window in which to peer in on their fellow visitors in the surrounding areas below. Like many prosperous seaside towns, the advent of cheaper package holidays had resulted in a decline in visitor numbers over the years. Despite this, the Isle of Man was able to retain, to a large extent, its proud heritage — including, as it happened, the unique structure perched precariously on the hillside.

Madeline sat in the passenger seat giving a series of overemphasised breaths to convey her impatience. "You know what, Joey? If you were looking for an alternative career, you could always be a driver for Miss Daisy?"

Joey looked out of the corner of his eye and resisted the temptation to lean across her, open the door, release her seatbelt, and throw her onto the road. "So you're saying I have the mellifluous voice of Morgan Freeman? Is that what you're trying to say?"

"I was referring to your leisurely pace!" Madeline countered.

"You want I should get arrested for speeding?" he said simply.

Abby leaned forward from the backseat just as they crossed over a bridge that spanned the attractive quay area of the island's capital, Douglas. "Just take a left here, Joey. Head for the breakwater over there," she said, pointing at a considerable concrete structure that kept the often-turbulent Irish Sea at bay. "Up there," she indicated. "That's the Camera Obscura."

"That's definitely where they're going to be?" asked Madeline. "My sister and your friend?"

Abby took a gulp. "Yes. Well, I think so. I can't imagine what else 'O C' might stand for. This must be it. It has to be."

Madeline stretched her neck for a better view, which, to Joey's frustration, meant her leaning across, over his line of sight. He once again resisted the urge to throw her bodily from the car.

"Are they not going to see us coming?" Madeline asked. "There's only one road and it's not exactly busy."

"I don't think they'd come this way," said Abby. "The usual way is up the main road. This way is an old tourist route, and it's unlikely they'd know to come this way. It certainly wouldn't be the route a satnav would send you," she explained. "Shit, Joey," she then added.

"Schmidt," he corrected her.

"Joey, I'm serious," she said. "Mr Esposito thinks that you've taken us to a secluded spot and that we're currently six feet under."

"Three feet," replied Joey. "I wouldn't have time, nor the inclination to go for six. What am I, an undertaker?"

The fragility of her life caused a shiver to run down Abby's spine. "Okay, granted, we're not worth the extra three feet. But the problem remains the same. If Mr Esposito sees us alive, he's going to kill you. We'll need to go in without you."

Joey thought for a moment. "If you two appear by yourselves, he'll kill you. Your only hope is if I come with you. Mikey will still hopefully be unconscious in the field. If not, I tied him up pretty tightly anyway, so he's going nowhere fast. Did you tell the police where to find him?"

Abby winced. "No, I forgot, what with everything going on and all. Madeline?"

"It wasn't exactly high on my priority list," Madeline admitted.

"Naw, it's fine. This probably helps," said Joey. "At this point, Mr Esposito still thinks I'm working for him."

"Out of curiosity, how do you go about resigning?" Madeline asked, with some cheek. "I mean, do you have a contract when you sign up to be a henchman? I know I've had jobs where I've had to give a month's notice before I could leave. Is it the same for you?"

"You know, it's funny you say that," Joey replied which a chuckle. "I've similar conversations with my partner. Well. Ex-partner."

"Do you have an annual appraisal?" Madeline continued. "You know. Where you get graded on how productive you've been over the previous year? Maybe how many people you've buried?"

It wasn't so funny anymore, then, and the mood turned sombre. "Mr Esposito," was all Joey said, "hopefully doesn't know that I've knocked Mikey out."

"What if he does?" asked Abby.

"Then we're all dead," replied Joey, matter-of-factly. Joey reached inside his jacket and took out his phone.

"What are you doing?" Abby asked.

"I'm phoning Mr Esposito," he replied, mashing the keypad as he pulled the car to the side of the road. He placed his finger to his lips. *"Shhh,"* he said. It was deathly quiet, so the ringtone echoed through the car.

After a half-dozen rings, it was picked upon the other end.

Joey cleared his throat. "Mr Swan? Mr Swan. Joey Schmidt reporting in to Mr Esposito. Where are you currently located, sir, if I may ask? Are you with Mr Esposito?"

Joey half-closed his eyes and scrunched up his face. He knew how precarious his current situation was. For all he knew, Mikey had escaped and was currently standing next to Mr Swan, filling him in on the day's events. In which case the current charade was all in vain.

Abby moved closer, but the thick flesh of Joey's ear muffled the speaker, preventing her eavesdropping.

Joey nodded his head as he listened intently. For someone who didn't overtly demonstrate signs of weakness, the bead of sweat that ran down his temple was evidence that Joey's underpants could soon be filled.

There was a pause and then Joey looked at the passenger seat, and then to the rear-view mirror, where the vision of Abby, chewing her lip, met him. "No, uh, Mr Swan. They're with me in the car," he related into his phone.

He listened once more, his eyes scouring the pretty vista around him as if seeking inspiration. "No, Mr Swan, they're very much alive, unfortunately, but they are still very much in my possession... Yes... Well...

Yes, I'm afraid we had a bit of an issue which prevented the instructions being carried out."

Madeline and Abby looked on intently.

"What went wrong?" Joey asked. His face contorted as the inspiration he sought eluded him. He looked at Abby and then over to Madeline for the glimmer of a suggestion, but, with none on offer, Joey was on his own.

He improvised. "The police pulled us over, Mr Swan," he offered, but it was fairly evident to the ladies that his acting skills were much like his digging skills: not entirely up to snuff. They shifted uncomfortably in their seats.

"Is, uh, Mikey with you, by any chance, Mr Swan?" asked Joey, as the bead of sweat now met up with his colossal neck.

The women leaned closer, anxious to see where this was leading, and what Joey could manage to pull out of his...

"Why would he be with you?" asked Joey. "Yes. About that. Here's the thing," he said, stalling, trying desperately to pull something out of his...

"Ass," he said. "He's an ass. Almost blew our whole operation. The police arrested Mikey, is what happened. So I hoped that maybe they'd have let him go and he'd be with you by now?"

Joey smiled as his confidence levels peaked.

"What did he get arrested for?" said Joey, crestfallen, his confidence once again leaving him. He tilted his head back, looking up to the heavens. His underpants suddenly became damp.

"Urinating. Urinating in the street," he said.

Joey looked in the rear-view mirror as Abby mouthed the words he'd just uttered back to him, with a look of utter despair on her face. Joey shrugged his shoulders.

"Yes, Mr Swan," he continued. "Mikey got out of the car to relieve himself, but he must have shaken it one too many times because the police arrested him for *outraging public decency*, I think they called it. As soon as the handcuffs came out I was gone, Mr Swan... Right... Yes... Most unfortunate, yes. So... where are you now? I suppose I should meet up for, uh... further instructions? I mean, considering the, uh... oh. Oh. Okay, then. Great... Yes... Yes, sir. Goodbye."

It was the most pathetic cover story ever told, but Mr Swan was either horrifically stupid or preoccupied because judging by the look of relief on Joey's face, the explanation had been accepted.

Joey collapsed back into the car seat, its springs creaking in protest. "Holy crap," he said. "Holy crap, I think he actually bought it!"

"And why wouldn't he?" said Madeline. "After all, it was all very convincing, an absolutely astonishing performance."

"It was?" asked Joey, well chuffed. "You really think so?"

Madeline appeared to roll one eye independently of the other. "No, Joey. I've seen better acting in a 70's porn film."

"Now what?" asked Abby, diverting Joey's attention away from the slight.

Joey refilled his lungs for a moment. "Well, your hunch was dead-on. Just as you suggested, they're meeting your sister at the Camera Obscura. At four p.m."

Abby gave him a *I-told-you-so* type of look, followed directly by a *and-you-doubted-me?* sort of look.

"Also," Joey went on. "It seems that your current status of being alive isn't as terrible as I'd thought."

"I should hope not!" interjected Madeline.

"You know what I mean," Joey told her. "Anyway, Mr Swan wasn't angry about it. He wants me to bring you both to him. They're meeting your sister," he said, nodding to Madeline. "And your friend," he said, looking to Abby through the rear-view (as it would have been difficult to turn his massive neck).

Abby nodded back at him. "They're still alive, then," she said, choking up. "Thank goodness."

"In twenty minutes," Joey stated. "So we need to get there first," he said. "There's a lighthouse nearby?" he asked.

Abby nodded. "Yes, it's near the Obscura. You can walk down to it, I think."

"Okay," said Joey. "That's where everyone is now. The men the two believe are FBI agents are going to meet them at the Obscura at four, as arranged, and then bring them back to the lighthouse."

"And what happens then?" asked Madeline, rather naïvely.

"I think," said Abby. "That anyone who can point a finger at Mr Esposito is going to meet with an unfortunate accident, very soon. With the proximity of the Irish Sea to that lighthouse, the clichéd watery grave would appear to be our final destination."

"So what the hell are we going there for?" asked Madeline. "We know they're going to hurt us. We came here to warn my sister and your friend. So let's just go do that and get the hell out!"

Abby nodded, as what Madeline said made sense. "You're right. But I don't know where Emma or Sam are going to be to warn them. The end meeting point is the Obscura, of course, but what I'm trying to say is that the only way to warn them is to walk into potential danger because there's no other way of knowing where they are, exactly. At least with Joey, he's got a gun. So we've got more hope. We've got to look on this as a positive.

About an hour ago, Joey and Mikey were going to bury us. So being above ground, as we are now, is actually a positive."

Abby added some 'jazz hands' along with her final statement but Madeline remained unconvinced. "I'm only going along with this insane, utterly ridiculous notion because there is no other way to save my sister," she responded.

"I'm well-armed," said Joey. "Now come on," he added, stepping out of the car. "You two look unhurt. If they see you looking like that, Mr Swan will know something is up. You need a couple of bruises."

"What?" said Madeline. "You're going to beat us up??"

Joey chuckled. "No," he said. "Believe me, if I were to beat you two up, you wouldn't be walking anywhere. No. *You're* going to beat yourselves up. Just hit each other a couple of times, that's all."

"What?" said Madeline, now stood on the pavement. "You want me and Abby to have a fight? I am *not* going to have a fight with Abby, that is absolutely—"

Abby had already jumped out of the car, however, and before Madeline had even known what hit her, Abby had thrown a right hook directly at Madeline's cheek. Her skin reddened immediately, and bruising shone through like a battered peach.

"What the hell!" said Madeline. "You actually just punched me!" she shouted, clutching at her cheek.

Abby bobbed on the spot. "I know, right? It's really liberating. Your turn."

Madeline looked like she'd seen a ghost. "I am absolutely not going to hit you, Abby. It is not ladylike, and it is not something I care to—"

Abby didn't wait for an invite and unleashed a left hook, catching Madeline on the opposing cheekbone. "Come at me, yo," said Abby, bobbing and weaving.

Madeline touched her face. "You hit me. *Twice,*" she said in disbelief.

"Yep. Bring it," Abby taunted her.

In response, Madeline flapped her hands in front of her face like a child swimming the doggy paddle — making contact with nothing but air.

The threat level for Abby was, at best, DEFCON 5 — least severe — and, realising this could go on perpetually, Abby obligingly leant forward and pressed her face into the flurry of hand movements that were now flailing quicker than a hummingbird's wings.

"There!" said Abby, nursing the onset of a graze on her cheek. "Will this do?" she asked of Joey.

"Yeah, whatever," said Joey walking away with a grin on his face.

Abby quickened her step to catch him up. "You didn't need us to roughen each other up, did you?"

"No," said Joey without hesitation. "It was fun to watch, though. I just wanted to see some girl-on-girl action. Now, come on, you two need to be in front of me looking intimidated once we get there. And make it look convincing. Otherwise, the three of us are going to end up in Davy Jones' locker."

They all climbed back into the car. "So… how many 70's porn films have you actually watched?" he asked a sulking Madeline sat in the passenger seat.

"Just drive!" both women shouted in unison.

Chapter Sixteen
Swanshead Revisited

Mr Swan admired the view from the foot of the lighthouse. There was no requirement for its services today as the sun bounced off the Irish Sea, which was as calm as a surgeon's hand. A silhouette of the west coast of England was clearly visible on the horizon. It was a staggeringly beautiful location and he was slightly melancholy, knowing it would be the nicest location he'd ever have a chance to commit murder, or at the very least, a serious maiming.

The temperature suited his stature, being that he was bordering on morbidly obese. The cooler Manx weather was less of a drain on his overworked sweat glands. He flicked his wrist out and glanced at his watch, and then took a moment to admire the marine birds that hovered overhead looking to snag an easy meal from the passing fishing boats.

He knocked on a substantial wooden door that was weathered — much like Mr Swan's own face — likely a result of being hammered by the salty sea air over the course of many years. Mr Swan's face, meanwhile, had presumably been weathered by other means.

"Tommy. Remo. It's time," he said, taking one final look at his watch.

The door opened shortly thereafter, and two men dressed identically all in black appeared.

"You two have been watching too many Will Smith films. It's going to your head."

"We're just getting into character, Mr Swan," said Tommy, standing on the right. "And, besides, it's Agent Weiss and Agent Tanner," he continued, pulling his fake identity card out of his pocket and flashing it for maximum impact.

"I'm happy you find this so entertaining, Agent Weiss. Don't mess this up," said Mr Swan, clearly unimpressed. "The boss wants this done quickly and done well. You need to meet the two of them and bring them back down here with no fuss."

"No problem, Mr Swan," said Remo, taking an admiring glance at his shimmering black shoes, straightening his tie, and then slipping on a pair of dark sunglasses. "How do I look?" he asked.

"Oh, just wonderful... Agent Tanner," said Mr Swan. "Now, gentleman. It's time."

Agent Weiss and Agent Tanner sauntered up the concrete steps that led to a coastal path.

"Hey! Did you just hit me?" asked Agent Tanner, taking a defensive stance.

"What? No, of course not," replied Agent Weiss. "If I was going to hit you, you'd know it was me because you'd be looking up at me, from down on the ground, where you'd be crawling around looking for your teeth."

"Or my contact lens. Remember that one time?" asked Agent Tanner.

Agent Weiss chuckled good-naturedly at his comrade-in-arms. "Yeah, that was funny. Good times," he said." He really did love his job.

"No, but seriously," said Agent Tanner. "I really did just feel something hit me."

"A guilty conscience?" suggested his partner.

"As if!" Tanner replied. And they both had a good laugh.

They carried on along the path cautiously; their FBI-issued footwear was not designed for the terrain, and, as such, navigating it presented something of a challenge. Steep steps took them down towards a picturesque beach. They didn't have time to stop and admire, however, as they faced another daunting set of steps which were narrower than the first.

Agent Weiss took a position to the rear, and he began to laugh.

"What's so funny now?" demanded Tanner.

The sniggering continued. "You know how you thought I hit you?" said Weiss.

"Yeah. Well, more of a flick, really," replied Tanner.

"Whatever. Anyway, I think I know who assaulted you," his partner answered, pointing.

Tanner stopped and arched his neck, struggling to get a view of his back. "What?" he said, getting frustrated. "What are you seeing? There's nothing there."

"Take off your jacket and look at it," said Weiss.

Tanner reluctantly agreed, although he kept a cautionary, distrustful eye on his partner as he followed through. They were always playing pranks on each other, so he had to be prepared for anything.

"Hey! You little feathery freaks!" he shouted at the sky. "That ain't right!"

A gull or similar winged assailant had expertly delivered its payload of poop on the back of the jacket, with the slick white crud appearing, in sharp relief, against the jet-black suit fabric.

Tanner took his gun from its holster and waved it furiously at any bird to fly within shooting distance. "You want a piece of this, you abominations of nature? Do ya??"

"Put your piece away, dumbass!" shouted Weiss. "If we get arrested before we even get to the rendezvous point, we're screwed!"

"What about my jacket?" Tanner protested. "It's ruined!" he pleaded.

"I dunno. Take it off and carry it under your arm?"

"What? But I've got a gun holstered under each arm. The jacket covers them up, so how am I gonna—?"

"So wear it, then!" replied Weiss. "What the hell do I care?"

"Little bastards," mumbled Tanner as he reluctantly holstered his gun. "And I didn't iron my shirt, either," he added.

"Huh?" Weiss responded.

Tanner brushed the front of his shirt with his hand. "I didn't iron it. Well, I did. I mean, the parts you can see, obviously," he explained. "But not the rest."

Weiss struggled to understand what he was hearing. "Wait, what? You only iron the front of your shirt? The part that's showing? But what if you need to take your jacket off?"

"Well I didn't plan on taking my jacket off today!" replied Tanner. "And doing it this way shaves about seven minutes off my getting-ready routine," he said happily, pleased to be able to impart this practical tip for his partner's benefit. "It's a real time-saver!"

"Great plan that turned out to be," said Weiss sceptically. "See, in our line of work, you gotta plan for the unexpected."

"Point taken," Tanner replied, grudgingly.

"So that's why I always iron my whole shirt," Weiss went on. "Because you just never know what..." he said, trailing off.

"Because you just never know what *what?*" Tanner asked.

"Dude. What the hell are you doing?" asked Weiss.

"How do you mean?" Tanner replied innocently.

"You're walking so close to me. Move up a little, for god's sake. If you stop short, I'm gonna plough you right in the ass! I mean, we're friends and everything. But, Christ. We're not *that* tight."

Tanner turned. "But, see, if I walk real close to you, then nobody will be able to see the mess on my back," he explained.

Weiss remained unmoved. "If you invade my personal space like that again, you'll need to worry about your white only-front-parts-ironed shirt being covered in *blood. Capisce?"*

Tanner sulked. "I guess. Well, everything except the *capisce* part. What does that even mean, anyway?"

"Forget about it," said Weiss. "Can you focus, please? We've got work to do."

A further set of steps greeted them, but the Camera Obscura was now visible near to the top.

"Ugh. You've got to be kidding me," said Tanner, when presented with the further climb, but they pressed on. "You know what? It's pretty, this Camera Obscura thing," he said after a few minutes of trudging, looking up at their goal and admiring the freshly-applied green paint on the wooden structure.

"Pretty?" said Weiss. "Dude. You're a ruthless killer, fercryinoutloud. Get some self-respect, man," he said to Tanner reprovingly.

"I was just saying. Jeez."

"Yeah, yeah. You're always *just saying."*

Once at their destination, the two men took up position at the entrance. Tactically, it was an ideal meeting point because it afforded views from all angles; the element of surprise would have been all but impossible. A further coastal path ran directly in front of them, which led from Douglas Head on the right, through to the headland on the left — which looked directly down on the lighthouse they'd just left.

"Ah!" said Tanner.

"What is it? You see them?" replied Weiss.

"No, my feet just hurt," Tanner called over. "No, wait. Over there!" he said, poised like a coiled spring. Or, bent over in pain. One or the other.

"Why are you reaching for your gun?" asked Weiss. "We're the good guys this time. If you pull your gun out on them, that's going to create a little confusion, don't you think? Save the bad guy stuff for when we throw their bodies into the sea."

"The bad guy stuff is my favourite part," said Tanner.

"Mine, too," agreed Weiss. "But they think they're coming to the FBI for help, remember?"

Tanner removed his hand cautiously like he was taking cheese from a mousetrap. "They're coming right for us. Is that them?"

Weiss squinted. "Dunno. Hard to tell from here. I only met the guy once. And this woman looks older than I remember. Are they armed?" he asked.

Two figures approached from the path on the left — a man and a woman. They both wore khaki shorts and matching blue rain jackets.

"I don't think that's them," Tanner said, once the couple got within range. "The guy looks like he's about eighty and the woman with him can't be much younger. Unless... maybe they're wearing disguises?"

"If those are disguises, they should be working in Hollywood," remarked Weiss. "No, that's just an old couple out for a walk."

The old couple approached the foot of the stairs and looked up to Weiss and Tanner. What Weiss had thought might be a weapon or weapons in hand was now clear to see were walking poles.

The old man looked at his walking companion. "The attendants dress very smart," he said, before chuckling for no obvious reason. "Two tickets!" His head was buried in his wallet as he shouted up. "Do you have concessions for pensioners?" he asked, earnestly.

Weiss had to put his arm across to Tanner as he was about to accept the money the old fellow was offering. "I'm sorry, sir, but we're closed today," he said to the pensioner.

"What's that?" shouted the elderly man.

"We're closed today," repeated Weiss. "So, you know, *bugger off,* as you folks might say."

The old man began to chuckle once more. "You'll have to forgive my hearing aid." His companion was likely his wife, judging by the way she tenderly held onto his arm. "How much did he say?" he asked of her.

She looked blankly. "What's that? I've told you, Bert, my batteries have gone," she said, pointing to her ear.

Bert continued to laugh. "We've not got one good ear between us!" he shouted amiably. He took a couple of notes from his wallet and held them out to Tanner. "Two tickets, please!" he repeated cheerily.

Tanner wanted very much to relieve the old fellow of his money. Force of habit, of course. Instead, he leaned forward, and, to ensure the message was understood, clearly and loudly enunciated the words, "We're closed. BURGER OFF."

Weiss sighed but did not correct his partner.

Bert, message finally received, reared up like a stallion. "There's no need to take that tone with me, young man." He took his walking stick and pointed it at the entrance sign. "You're clearly open for another hour," he insisted, poking his stick in the air for emphasis. "We've walked for an hour to come to this, so take my money and step aside before I'm forced to give you a proper thrashing!"

"We're closed," said Tanner, opening his jacket to reveal that which lay within. No further words were necessary.

Bert's wife pulled at his jacket. "I don't like this, Bert. Let's go," she shouted into his ear.

Agent Tanner did his best to look intimidating.

"Ruffians," Bert said, turning to his wife with a stern expression over his face. "I've met their kind before. Let's be on our way."

While his wife could not hear him, she understood well enough and turned to leave. Bert did the same, dropping down one of the steps and extended his walking pole for support. But then, suddenly...

"A-ha!" Bert shouted. With the precision of a master swordsman, he spun on the spot and landed the tip of his pole deep into Tanner's crotch.

"No fair!" screamed Tanner as he fell to his knees. The air flew out of his lungs and the blood drained from his face. He looked up at Weiss for salvation, but as he tried to ease back into an upright position, Bert unleashed another savage salvo, this time catching Tanner across the chest.

"Help me," pleaded Tanner, but Weiss had by now taken a cautionary step back as tears of laughter rolled down his face.

Aware of another impending attack, Tanner tried to distance himself, but his legs had stopped working as the pain in his crotch became overwhelming. He could only use his arms to drag himself away from the wrinkly aggressor. His escape was unimpressive, and had the appearance of a dog trying to scratch its arse on the carpet.

"Okay, okay," said Weiss, eventually deciding enough was enough. He took a step towards Bert and raised his hands in submission. "Look, we're open, like you've said, but we've had an unfortunate incident inside."

Bert remained poised to attack but moved his head closer as Weiss continued.

"Yeah, sadly some old fellow slipped and broke his neck. The floor is a bit, you know, wet and slippery and such now. From the blood."

"Oh, dear. He's dead?" asked Bert.

"Yeah," said Weiss. "He's going nowhere, unfortunately."

"Oh, dear," Bert said again, trying to look towards the building, but Weiss blocked his view. "So what are you two doing?" he asked, undaunted.

"Us?" said Weiss. "We, uh... we're the undertakers. Why else do you think we'd be dressed like this, up here, in the middle of the day?"

"Ah," said Bert. "Ah. Well. I'm sorry to hear that. I think we'll be on our way, then."

Tanner continued to gasp on the floor. "Yeah, you *better* go," he mumbled through gritted teeth. "If you know what's good for you. If you don't want a visit from the undertakers yourself."

Weiss helped his fallen colleague back to his feet as Bert and his wife continued their exploration.

"You just got decked by a senior citizen. Priceless," said Weiss, thoroughly enjoying the moment. But his laughter dried up when he looked and saw a couple walking toward them at speed. "This must be them!" he whispered.

Tanner tried to focus through the tears. "The guy we saw in the office was bald, wasn't he?"

"Yeah, you're right. But that's definitely her," said Weiss.

This was confirmed as the pair in question walked nearer the Camera Obscura.

"You're late," said Weiss to Emma. "Who's he?" he said, pointing to Sam.

Sam waved. "Hiya. It's me. Sam. We met in my office. What's wrong with your partner?"

"He ate some bad, uh... fish and chips," Weiss floundered.

"You're wearing a wig?" asked Tanner. "Why?"

"I dunno, but I think a bald head makes me stand out, so I wanted to remain inconspicuous," Sam replied.

Emma scoffed. "Inconspicuous? Is that what that was?"

Sam blushed. "Yeah, our discreet arrival didn't really go to plan. I didn't have the right wig adhesive, so I used treacle. It's a thing I seem to keep doing. You'd think I'd learn," he said.

"But, no," Emma added.

"Anyway," Sam continued. "That's why we're a bit late. See, I've just been dive-bombed by a load of hungry seagulls. Who knew they'd like treacle? But, hey, at least the wig is still in place, right?"

Tanner nodded. "I feel your pain. Check out my jacket," he said, twirling like a ballerina. "Those gulls ruined it!"

Sam nodded. "They're merciless little bastards," he said sympathetically.

Agent Tanner seemed pleased he no longer had to hide his soiled jacket. At least that problem was solved.

Agent Weiss took a step forward and stared at Emma. "You weren't followed?" he asked.

Emma shook her head.

"You've made the right decision to come to us, Emma. You're prepared to make a full confession about your dealings with Mr Esposito? Including details of all the artwork and artefacts you've forged?"

Emma nodded once more. "Yes, I'll tell you everything. You just need to get me off this island and into witness protection or something."

"You do realise that your life as you knew it is about to change? Forever?" offered Agent Tanner.

"I understand, Agent...?"

"Tanner," said Agent Tanner.

"Agent Tanner. I just wanted to say thank you to you both. So. Now what? What happens next?"

Weiss looked over his shoulder. "We've got our operations centre in an old lighthouse, just at the bottom of the cliff. It's only a five-minute walk."

Emma looked at Sam with an air of vulnerability. "Sam," she said, standing on tiptoe. "I also want to thank you. For everything. Especially for getting me here today. To safety."

Sam frowned. "I'm coming with you," he said. "And that's that. I'm seeing this through."

Emma glanced at the two agents who in turn looked at each other. "Does he know the full details of your dealings with Mr Esposito?" asked Tanner.

"Absolutely," replied Emma, without hesitation.

"Well, welcome aboard," offered Tanner, a crooked smile across his face. "Let's roll," he said, and ushered them down the steps and towards the quaint-looking lighthouse. "Emma, don't panic, by the way. You're with the professionals now," he added reassuringly. "You'll be taken care of.

Chapter Seventeen
Fall of the House of Joey

Madeline arched her back and walked uncomfortably, like she was struggling to retain the contents of her bowels. "That better be your gun pointing in my back, Joey," she said. "God, that's a phrase I never thought I'd utter."

Joey stood behind the two women with a gun pointed at each of them. Ever the professional, it was as if he'd bought a clothing line designed to provide a covering for small-arms fire. His jacket sleeves perfectly obscured the contents of his hands from prying eyes.

"Just go with it," said Joey through the corner of his mouth. "We don't know if we're being watched, and it needs to look like you're being brought here against your will. So look, um… aggrieved and, uh… in distress. Or something."

"How am I supposed to…?" Madeline muttered to herself, before Joey applied more pressure on her back, and, like magic, her acting skills improved immediately. "That hurts," she moaned.

"Perfect. That's the spirit," said Joey. "Abby, is this the lighthouse?"

This was a question one might charitably say was rhetorical (or, uncharitably, stupid), bearing in mind they were in the middle of nowhere with a forty-foot structure with a giant light at the top. Abby resisted the urge to give a snarky response. After all, she had a loaded gun secured at the base of her back. "It is indeed. You've got a keen eye, Joey," she replied diplomatically (though perhaps with a bit of snark thrown in for good measure). "Joey, the gun pressed against my back. Is it loaded?"

"It is indeed, Abby," he said, playfully matching her words and style. "Don't worry, I know what I'm doing with a gun."

"That's what I'm afraid of," Abby replied.

There were several buildings surrounding the foot of the lighthouse, but there were no signs of life. Joey's eyes were wide, like golf balls, as he scoured the location for any sign of Mr Esposito or his ample-of-girth assistant Mr Swan. "It might be a trap," he whispered. "If I say run, don't ask. Just run."

Joey moved forward a step as the sound of an aged lock mechanism being undone echoed through the still air. He didn't hesitate and raised the two guns so they stood in the air at the ten-and-two position, at the ready.

"If I don't see some faces, soon, I'm going to start unleashing a whole lotta lead," he said, gravely.

A bloated face appeared from behind a door in the far corner of the small courtyard. "Joey," said Mr Swan, who knew better than to challenge a gun-wielding Joey Schmidt. "Over here. Quickly, before anybody sees you."

Joey nodded in acknowledgement and took a large breath. "If this is a double-cross," he whispered to the women. "I'll jump in front of you and you both run. No matter what, don't look back," he instructed.

Mr Swan ushered them in, took a cautionary glance beyond them, scanning the cliffs above, before slamming the door shut. The room looked like something from a pirate's tavern — with every element of tacky, nautical souvenir adorning the walls.

Mr Esposito spun around on an impressive captain's chair, once again sporting his familiar white linen suit.

Madeline laughed. It was not a kindly sort of laugh. She spoke directly to Mr Esposito. "You've got to be kidding me. Seriously? How long have you been sitting in that chair, staring at the wall, waiting for us to arrive, just so you could spin around like a second-rate Bond villain? The only thing you're missing is the white cat."

Mr Esposito smiled. "No cats. Allergies, I am afraid. It is enjoyable to make your acquaintance once again, Marilyn."

"It's Madeline," Madeline scowled. "And you know it."

"Ah. My sincere apologies," said Mr Esposito. "A simple mistake," he said, unconvincingly. "Mr Schmidt, any news on our Mr Montgomery?"

Joey lowered his head slightly, in an attempt to avoid direct eye contact. "Mikey? Uh, no, sir," he answered. "I thought he'd be back with you by now. You... haven't heard from him?"

"No," said Mr Swan, stepping forward. "In fact, we hoped you might be able to clear things up in that respect." Mr Swan stood nose-to-nose with Joey, his nostrils flaring.

"No, Mr Swan, it's like I said, the police took him away for getting a little too familiar with himself in public. He always was, like they say around these parts, a bit of a wan–"

"That will do, Mr Schmidt," said Mr Esposito. "After all, we're in the presence of two ladies. Two ladies I had not expected to see again, to be completely honest. But, no matter. The inconvenience with Mr Montgomery being arrested has actually turned out to be to our advantage."

"That's... good?" asked Joey. "It's just... I hate to disappoint you, sir. I prefer to complete an assignment as instructed, of course."

"Not at all," replied Mr Esposito, soothingly. "Quite the opposite. We are waiting patiently for Madeline's sister, at present, and I need to know exactly what she's told and to whom. I have a number of business associates who are exceptionally interested in the outcome of this meeting."

"Yes, sir," said Joey.

"Some of these associates are, as you may imagine, somewhat nervous that Madeline's sister has been fairly liberal with her knowledge of our operations of late. This information has the potential to separate my associates, as well as myself, from their liberty. You can understand, of course, if I prefer such a chain of events were not to occur."

"Of course," Joey agreed, biding his time, waiting to see how this was all going to play out.

"Our Emma Hopkins, however, may prove reluctant to divulge the information we are seeking," he went on.

"You're damn right!" Madeline interjected.

"Precisely," Mr Esposito continued. "And this is why having Madeline here as our guest can prove to be of benefit. Because, while Ms Hopkins may not be willing to cooperate for her own sake, I am confident that the application of a persuasive degree of pressure on her sister's person may produce the desired results."

If Mr Esposito had been holding a cat, he would have, at this point, been stroking it affectionately.

"She'll tell you nothing!" snapped Madeline.

"I certainly hope so, beautiful. I'm counting on it," Mr Swan said, withdrawing his attention from Joey for the moment and focussing now on Madeline. "I'm looking forward to making a mess of this pretty face of yours. Although," he said, caressing Madeline's face with the back of his chubby hand. "Although someone's already got a head start, from the looks of it."

"That'd be me," said Abby willfully, as she shadow-boxed a feigned left and right hook. "And you're next, tubby," she added, defiantly.

Joey winced at Abby's admission, which could very well raise questions that he didn't have the ability to easily answer. Fortunately, Mr Swan provided a timely and welcome distraction in the form of his phone ringing.

Mr Swan took his phone from his pocket and glanced at the display. "They're on their way, Mr Esposito," he said eagerly. "And they're not alone."

"Very fine," said Mr Esposito. "Very fine."

Two porthole-shaped windows provided the only illumination into the murky room. A large model anchor in the courtyard cast an impressive shadow on the rear wall. Abby stooped down to get a better view of the figures moving up the winding path. Her heart thumped when she caught a glimpse of Sam.

"No. Sam," she said, biting her cheek. She started to move towards the window, but Mr Swan grabbed the back of her hair and yanked her back into place.

Joey had to resist the urge to crush the back of Mr Swan's skull with his gun.

"That's far enough, sweetheart," said Mr Swan. "We don't want them two to see you just yet."

Abby struggled against his hold, but Mr Swan casually parted his jacket with his free hand to reveal his weapon. "Temper, temper," he admonished her.

Madeline clenched her fists. She knew she had to do something, but just didn't know what. In desperation, she leaned down and grabbed for a heavy ceramic octopus which sat, legs splayed, on the floor, offering itself as a doorstop.

She swung it and missed Mr Swan's head by inches, but his head was not the intended target. When released, it hurtled through the air like a missile, torpedoing the glass porthole like a, well, like a multi-armed ceramic mollusc through a porthole. Before Mr Swan had time to react, Madeline screamed, "Emma, run! It's a trap!"

Mr Swan grabbed his gun and thrust it under Madeline's chin. "One more word, sweetheart, and they'll need a mop to soak what's left of you up."

Brave as she was, the presence of a gun so close to her face was enough to silence her.

Mr Esposito stood with urgency. "Mr Swan?" he said.

Mr Swan needed no further instruction. He moved towards the broken window. "It's fine, boss," he said. "The guys have got it under control."

Moments later, figures moved in front of the one remaining intact window, disrupting the perfect shadow on the wall and replacing it with an even larger, more ominous shadow.

Agents Tanner and Weiss forced Sam and Emma through the doorframe at gunpoint.

"Smashing welcome," said Tanner, in reference to the broken window.

His partner looked at him uncertainly. *"Smashing?* Really? You're talking like the locals now?"

"Well, when in Rome," replied Tanner, shrugging his shoulders.

Weiss shook his head, disappointed.

Abby lurched forward, as much as she was able. "Sam!" she shouted. "They're not the FBI!"

Sam smiled. "Yeah, I pretty much got that when he stuck a gun in my back. Are you okay?" he asked.

"What a delightful little reunion," announced Mr Esposito. "Quite the gathering," he said, moving towards Emma. He stood in front of her and smiled. "The wonderfully talented, Emma. We had a wonderful thing going, did we not we?" he asked.

"We did not," was Emma's response. She struggled, trying to release her arms from Weiss's grip, but to no avail.

"Oh, but I think we did," Mr Esposito went on. "A shame you had to spoil it," he said. "Such a shame. Tell me, Emma, I know you have spoken to the FBI. The real FBI, that is. I need to know what you have told them, my dear."

"Like hell I'll tell you," cursed Emma, flicking her head in disgust.

"I think, perhaps, you will." Mr Esposito gave a gentle laugh, then turned to his associate. "Mr Swan, if you would be kind enough, please?"

"Sure thing, boss. Been waiting for this," was Mr Swan's response, and he grabbed Madeline by the neck and began to squeeze.

It was horrible to watch. Madeline's eyes started to water, and her face reddened as she gasped for air like a fish caught on the beach at low tide.

"That's enough!" shouted Joey, moving his considerable frame towards Mr Swan.

Mr Esposito motioned to his associate with a flourish of his hand, and the grip on Madeline's neck was released. Mr Swan appeared displeased at having to do so, but of course he complied.

Mr Esposito walked over to Joey. "It would seem you are developing a curious trace of compassion, Mr Schmidt," he suggested. "Perhaps not the best trait in our line of work."

Joey took a step back and lowered his shoulders. "No, sir," he replied. "No, it's not that."

Mr Esposito paced around Joey, looking him up and down. "Yes, I fear you are losing your touch, Mr Schmidt. We need her to speak," he said, looking at Emma Hopkins, before continuing. "So, Mr Schmidt, I would like you to use the neck of Ms Hopkins' sister here, in such a way as to make Ms Hopkins talk, if you would be kind enough. After all, you have just assured me that, contrary to my supposition, you have not, in fact, lost your touch."

"Yes, sir," Joey had no choice but to reply. The blood drained from his face as he stepped forward. He knew that disobeying Mr Esposito was a death sentence. He betrayed no emotion as he raised his right hand to her throat. And squeezed.

"Joey, no, you can't do this!" shouted Abby. "This isn't you anymore!" she pleaded.

Joey turned to Abby, but his face was impassive as stone as his hold tightened further. The heel of Madeline's shoe flapped to the floor as the grip on her throat raised her up on tiptoe. She gurgled, and her eyes looked like they were on stalks, ready to pop out of her head.

Mr Esposito gave a satisfied smile when Madeline looked to her sister imploringly to relieve her suffering. "You can make this all go away, Ms Hopkins," Mr Esposito told Emma. "This need not continue."

In a blur of motion, Joey had released his grip on Madeline and his hand was reaching inside his jacket.

Unfortunately, Mr Swan was ready for this. "Ah-ah-ah," he said, pressing the muzzle of his gun against the side of Joey's head. "And what do you need a gun for, Joey?"

Mr Swan gave a glance to one of the other two henchmen — who up until now had done nothing, standing like bookends awaiting instruction. Mr Swan gave a nod, and Bookend №1 left the room via the front door, taking care to avoid the shards of glass from the broken window scattered across the floor.

Mr Swan reached inside Joey's jacket and removed his gun. "I'm not convinced you were going to shoot *her*, Joey, so the only other option is that you were going to shoot *us*. Is that what you thought you were going to do, Joey?" sneered Mr Swan.

Mr Swan frisked Joey. There was nothing else to be found in the jacket, so attention was shifted to the legs. Mr Swan smirked as he lifted Joey's trouser leg, first on the left and then on the right, revealing a gun tucked away nicely on each ankle. "I thought as much," said Mr Swan. "You don't mind?" he asked, relieving Joey of his weapons. "Then again, it really wouldn't matter if you *did* mind, would it?"

Joey's concerns about the current situation were confirmed when Bookend №1 re-entered the room with a smug grin plastered across his face.

Mr Swan kept his gun trained on Joey's head. "I've got someone eager to meet you, Joey!" he said, barely able to contain his excitement. And then he nodded to the underling again.

Bookend №1 stood to one side and a familiar figure filled the doorframe.

Joey gave a resigned laugh, but he felt like he'd been kicked in the stomach. He looked at Madeline and Abby and shook his head before turning back to the door.

"Not as smart as you thought, are you, Schmidt?" said Mikey Montgomery, entering the room.

"Mikey," said Joey, facing his former partner. "That's some lump on your face," he said with a crooked frown. "I wish now that I'd given you another."

Mikey rubbed his face. "You should have, Joey. It might have saved your life," he replied, and he advanced towards Joey, fist cocked.

"No, not yet," said Mr Swan, placing a hand across Mikey's chest. "Not quite yet. I understand your eagerness. But we have some business to attend to first."

A small blood vein pulsated on Mikey's forehead. He was like a caged bull desperate to be let loose, although, without a gun pointed at his person, Joey could easily have wiped the floor with him.

"Enough of the distractions," said Mr Esposito. "As much as I have enjoyed my stay on this little island, my time here is coming to an end. I have a bottle of Italian brandy waiting for me on my jet. *Squisito.* And I really should not leave it unattended much longer. I am sure you understand."

Emma raised her hands in submission. "Mr Esposito, I'll continue to work for you," she insisted. "You always said I was the best forger in the business. I'll do whatever you need. Make you whatever you need. I'll make you rich."

"Ah, but I am already wealthy, Ms Hopkins," he replied.

"Please, Mr Esposito. I've forged, what, over a hundred items for you? I'll do more. Anything. Just let us all go. Please," she said, her cheeks awash with tears. "I promise I won't talk to anyone. Please don't kill us."

Mr Esposito smiled sunnily. He placed his hands in his jacket pockets amiably. It was at times like these that he wished he were not allergic to cats. It would have given him something to do with his hands.

"It is certainly true that you have added a number of zeros to my account balances, Ms Hopkins. However, I know that you have already spoken to the authorities. And, regardless of how much money I may have, it would be of no use to me should I be serving thirty years' time in some prison, now would it?"

Emma opened her mouth to protest, but it was futile.

"I am afraid we are well beyond the point of you pleading for your life having any effect whatsoever, my dear. My business partners would find it fantastically distressing if I were to let you go. If I were to let *any* of you go."

Joey's eyed danced around the room, calculating any advantage. At present, there was none.

"Emma Hopkins," Mr Esposito went on, almost gently. "I have relished my time working with a master such as yourself, but the simple fact of the matter is that I cannot afford for you to testify against me. What I must do, you understand, is nothing personal. It is simply a business decision. As you must know, I do not hesitate to, shall we say, *disassociate myself,* from those who put my operations at risk. I regret to say that today I find it necessary to disassociate myself from an additional four people."

"Five people," Mr Swan interrupted impertinently.

"Mr Swan?" Mr Esposito responded politely, ever unflappable.

"Don't forget Joey, boss," Mr Swan suggested, tapping his gun against Joey's beefy arm.

Mr Esposito raised one hand in acquiescence. "Ah, quite right, Mr Swan. And what would I ever do without you?"

Mr Swan bowed his head in gratitude.

"Has the boat arrived?" Mr Esposito enquired, turning to the second bookend.

"Yes," responded Bookend №2, pleased to be called upon for the first time ever.

"Very fine," said Mr Esposito, replacing his familiar cream fedora hat. "Now. I am terribly sorry to have to say *addio* to you all," he announced, with an impressive air of sincerity. "But, I have business elsewhere. There is some good news for you, however," he added. "At least you are going to go on a nice little boat trip. Most unfortunately, you will not be enjoying it for very long."

Emma reached out like she was making one last plea for her life. "Mr Esposito. To confirm. You're going to kill us? The five of us? Like you've killed so many others?"

Mr Esposito smiled wanly. He looked at Tanner and Weiss and paused for a moment. "Please tell me that you two have searched them?" he said in a manner that indicated he already suspected the answer.

Tanner and Weiss looked at each other like two schoolboys who'd been caught lighting the neighbour's pet on fire. Again.

"Sonnuva–" cursed Mr Swan, tearing toward Sam. He ripped open Sam's shirt, buttons popping off, each in turn, and sailing to the floor. "He's wired, boss," confirmed Mr Swan, and, with that, began pummelling whoever was closest to him — which, unfortunately for Agent Tanner, was him.

The smile never left Mr Esposito's face, as he took a cursory glance through the remaining intact portal window. "Well done, Emma. Truly excellent. Although this only brings the timing of your demise forward, I fear." He made for the door and turned to Mr Swan just as he reached it. "Kill them all," he told him. "Now."

"Shit!" someone shouted.

"It's SCHMIDT!" Joey Schmidt yelled. And, with that rallying cry, he came to life.

He threw a right hook at Weiss that all but removed his head from his shoulders.

Tanner jumped into the fray, but was blinded from the tears of pain welled up in his eyes from Mr Swan's clobbering and soon greeted the floor with his face.

The two bookends were about to earn their wages as they reached inside their jackets to carry out Mr Esposito's order. But, before they could act, Sam swung his left foot and caught Bookend №1 squarely in the bollocks. Bookend №1 fell to his knees with a whimper, and then promptly passed out from the pain.

Bookend №2 moved back, out of the way of his fallen comrade, and managed to release a shot from his pistol.

Sam winced, closing his eyes as he threw a punch with everything he had in the locker. He opened his eyes in time to watch his clenched fist make contact with the offending chin. Bookend №2's eyes rolled back in his head as he crashed against a painted jolly roger mural hung on the wall.

Sam didn't have a moment to revel in his knockout punch as the sound of another shot deafened him a moment before the smell of burning gunpowder filled the air.

"Joey!" screamed Madeline, and rushed to his aid. She cradled Joey's head as he lay the floor. "Joey!" she screamed once more, in horror, seeing the palms of her hands now covered in blood.

Mr Swan swung round and pointed his gun directly at Sam. Mr Swan smiled for an instant before the sound of a gunshot rang out, once more.

"Sam! Oh, no!" pleaded Abby. Sam stood motionless with a simple expression on his face. He didn't speak as he clutched his chest. He gave Abby the gentlest glimmer of a smile as he staggered back. "I'd catch... a lobster... for you..." he said before his head dropped.

"Don't you dare leave me, Sam Levy, don't you dare!" she demanded, reaching out to support him.

This all played out in a matter of moments. Mr Esposito had momentarily hesitated, but then he remembered himself and grabbed for the door.

"Mr Swan. If you please," he said. "Finish the job and kill the rest of them. We've outstayed our welcome."

There was no answer.

"Mr Swan."

Again, there was no answer.

Neither was there any further sound of gunfire.

Mr Esposito looked back, on the verge of chastising his faithful assistant, but saw Mr Swan fallen to the floor, wobbling on one knee, and gasping.

Mr Swan looked up at Mr Esposito, holding the palm of his right hand to his heart, as if swearing an oath. Blood seeped through his fingers. "Boss. I'm sorry, boss..." he said, before falling face-first onto the cold concrete floor.

The sound of footsteps echoed through the courtyard as the outline of several new shadows flitted across the rear wall.

"Nobody move!" screamed a figure, gun drawn, emerging in the smoke-filled room. He was followed closely by several more armed men, awaft in the smoky haze, who repeated the same instructions but with even more ferocity.

But nobody was moving.

Many were down for the count. Of those remaining, Abby was holding onto Sam and Madeline cradled Joey on the floor.

Only Mr Esposito was standing, and that wasn't for long as he was quickly dispatched.

As the smoke spilt out of the opened door and the room cleared, Emma stared at the lead figure looming over them, his face now revealed. She stared at him but she couldn't seem to work out what she was seeing.

"Henry? Henry, is that you?"

None of the armed men waivered. "Search everyone," demanded one of them. "If anyone moves, take them down," he said. "I want everyone restrained until we figure out who's who in this godforsaken mess."

Madeline looked up at the armed men with tears in her eyes. "You need to help me," she pleaded. "I think we're losing Joey."

Chapter Eighteen
Blood, Treacle & Tears

The Isle of Man was, on the whole, a rather sedate, picturesque place to live, and an idyllic place to visit. It was this charming allure that brought Sam to the little island in the middle of the Irish Sea all those years ago. For a place with a minimal crime rate, the sight that greeted those enjoying the sun-kissed Douglas Beach that day would live long in their memories. It was a scene better suited to a Tom Clancy novel than a seaside town as three helicopters appeared from their cover behind the rolling Manx hills. A Navy gunship filled Douglas Harbour from where several ribs were dispatched, heading at speed towards the lighthouse sat precariously on the cliff.

All roads in and out of the island's capital were closed as inquisitive onlookers gathered on the periphery, drawn by the thumping noise from the helicopters which circled the bay.

"You have to help him," said Madeline, as the paramedic eased her gently to one side.

"We'll do what we can, I promise," said the man with a face that oozed compassion. "Give him some room, please. We need space to work. Now, what's his name?" he asked to Madeline.

"Joey," she said.

"And his surname?" he asked.

Madeline looked blankly. "I don't think we know, do we?" she asked, looking around the room. "I mean, for certain? We don't even know if Joey is his real name. But he answers to Joey."

"Joey it is, then," the man said as he started examining his patient.

Armed police filled the room and any movement was closely scrutinised. Two officers stood over Mr Swan as another paramedic worked furiously on him as well. She looked exhausted when she eventually looked up at the two officers. "There's nothing more I can do. This one's gone," said the medic. She said this dejectedly, but also with acceptance as this, unfortunately — as a paramedic — came with the territory.

Having prioritised her workload, and once Mr Swan was confirmed dead, the paramedic moved her attention to Sam — who sat with his back against the wall with Abby gently holding his hand.

Sam's wig had worked its way loose, though Abby had thoughtfully pressed it back in place. But the sweat from his forehead, mixed with the sweet sugary glue, congealed on his forehead. The female paramedic knelt on one knee beside him. Her attention was immediately drawn to the foreign substance.

"Code, em... *rubbish!*" she shouted to her colleague. "What's the code for a chemical attack??" she enquired, with great urgency.

"No, no, it's fine," Abby assured her. "It's just glue. From his wig."

The paramedic looked at her like Abby was speaking a foreign language.

Abby could understand the confusion as she wasn't much more the wiser than the befuddled face looking back at her.

"He wears a wig. When he's undercover," Abby explained. "But he doesn't have the right glue. Look," she said, rubbing her finger in the sugary, sweating mess. "It's treacle or syrup," she said, licking her finger with a mild look of disgust.

"Stand down on the chemical attack," said the paramedic to her colleagues. "But you may want to get in touch with the mental health team." She looked Sam up and down, and, as he was conscious, she moved her head closer. "Where were you shot?" she asked.

Sam looked at Abby for strength. "I don't know, Doctor, but I don't think I can feel my right leg." Sam raised his hands and showed a small trickle of blood running down the back of his hand, which caused Abby to place her own hand to her face in shock.

"I need you to stay calm," said the paramedic as she skillfully and efficiently moved over every inch of Sam's body. She moved her hand towards Sam's right leg and as she pressed on his calf muscle, he couldn't take the pain and screamed out.

"Will I lose the leg, Doctor?" asked Sam, his voice trembling.

"Be brave," said Abby, stroking his sticky head.

"I'm not a doctor. I'm a paramedic," said the paramedic. "But we'll do the best we can."

Sam closed his eyes, bracing himself against the terrible news he was certain to receive.

The paramedic leaned forward, resting on her knee. "Now, you did say you were shot?" she asked. "I'd just like to confirm?"

Sam nodded bravely. "Yes. Yes, I have," he replied, giving Abby a piteous glance.

"No. No, you haven't," said the paramedic. She rolled up Sam's right trouser leg and ripped a piece of Velcro clean off his skin. "This is what's causing you the pain," she said, holding up a gun holster that'd been attached to his leg. "You've had this fastened too tight on your leg. It's cut the circulation off, which is why you're in discomfort. She took a closer look at the gun, before removing it from its holster with an expression of consternation. "This gun..." she said, taking a second glance to make certain. "Is a plastic children's toy gun. Of the cowboy variety, in fact. If I'm not mistaken?" She held it aloft for inspection.

"You got that right, *pardner*," confirmed one of the officers at hand.

"What?" said Abby, removing her hand from the manufactured hairpiece. "He's not been shot? What about the blood?"

"Let me see your hand," said the paramedic, taking a careful glance. "There's a small shard of glass," she said, pinching it between her fingernails and plucking it free. "Likely from that broken glass. But he's fine," she said. "More or less," she added, pushing herself to her feet and moving off quickly to tend to someone else who might actually need some tending to.

Sam pressed his hands all over his body to verify the diagnosis, and to his great relief there were no holes save those he'd not woken up with that same morning. "So I won't be losing the leg?" he said to himself (since the medic had already buggered off).

Abby closed one eye, deep in thought, before looking at Sam. "Hang on. There's something I'm trying to work out here."

"I won't be losing the leg," Sam replied, sounding almost disappointed.

"Sam," she said. "There were only two bullets fired, yeah?" she said.

"Were there?" Sam answered. "Yes, I suppose you're right."

"So how is it that you thought you'd been shot? If there were only two shots fired. Because Joey received one bullet, right? And Mr Swan the other. And, also, why the hell am I still here caressing that mess that's stuck to your head?" she said, using Sam's own shirt to wipe her hand clean of the goo.

Sam looked like he was deep in thought. Or maybe constipated. One or the other. "Ah," he said, after a fashion. "Ah. Well." He coughed.

"Yes?" she asked expectantly, taking on the tone of a schoolmarm once again.

"Maybe I thought it was shrapnel?" he offered unconvincingly. "In all the, em, excitement? And, erm... confusion?"

Abby shook her head as Sam rose to his feet. He did so uneasily, for effect.

"And what the hell is with you having a gun holster with a plastic gun? What exactly were you playing at? What did you think you were you going to do with it? It doesn't do anything!"

Sam took it from her with a pained expression. "It does so do something," he insisted. "It's a cap gun," he said, pulling the trigger, releasing a rather pathetic pop noise that would barely have scared a fly off a fresh turd.

Abby's shoulders start to wobble, like jelly. Tears filled her eyes before spilling over onto her cheeks. Sam had seen this before. She was furious with him. Or, she was very distraught. One or the other. Either way, he felt certain she was about to explode in one way or another.

"I thought you'd been shot and you were going to die," she said miserably.

This wasn't what Sam had been expecting.

"And the only thing wrong was a splinter," she continued.

"A huge hunk of glass, it was," Sam interjected. "Very large indeed. Deadly large."

"...And a gun holster you'd fastened too tightly."

"I very nearly lost my leg," he offered helpfully.

She walked forward a pace and threw her arms around him. "I thought I'd lost you!" she cried.

Sam cautiously placed a reciprocal arm around her.

"Sam," said Abby through the tears. "If you're going to wear the wig, promise me you'll get proper glue. All I can taste and smell is syrup laced with your salt sweat."

"Okay?" was all he was able to muster under the circumstances.

"Now come on," she said, taking him by his good hand. "Let's see if we can't get out of here. I need a seriously large gin and tonic."

Chapter Nineteen
Vauxhalla

One month later...

Early evening in Peel on a warm summer's eve was splendid. The sound of children screaming with joy on the beach couldn't help but bring a smile to even the sternest of faces. Ice cream vendors were doing a roaring trade, closely followed by the bucket and spade vendors. Abby stood in front of Eyes Peeled, and she leaned comfortably against one of the windowsills outside work absorbing the panorama before her. There wasn't anywhere on earth she'd rather live, but she still felt slightly out of place wearing her finest black dress when most around were in shorts and t-shirt.

Regardless of her attire, however, she was never entirely off-duty. She was a PI, after all — a private dick, if you will, though of course, in her case, minus the dick — and she couldn't help but notice things. Like the clapped-out Vauxhall Astra on view, and it having driven up and down the promenade a number of times in a short span of time.

There were plenty of parking spaces available though the driver of the Vauxhall ignored all of them, and the occupants stole furtive glances in Abby's general direction as they drove slowly by again and again first one way and then the other.

She was immaculate having just had her hair styled and her makeup professionally applied, and in a moment of paranoia she wondered if the male passengers had perhaps mistaken her for a hooker brazenly plying her trade. Or, if indeed, there were something rather more nefarious going on given the circle of underworld figures she and Sam had dealt with only recently? Was an associate of Mr Esposito come to exact revenge?

Then again, would criminals of Mr Esposito's ilk arrive in a shabby Vauxhall Astra? It hardly seemed their style. Still, by now, Abby had learned to expect the unexpected and take nothing at all for granted.

The mysterious automobile came close once more, and this time it finally came to a stop — pulling over directly in front of the detective agency. The driver threw open his door, exiting the vehicle, and two more men spilt out from the rear.

Abby froze. She looked for an exit but there was none. She wore heels that were higher than a junkie on benefit day and would have made a rapid escape virtually impossible. The driver reached back into the car and pulled out a black case. Abby wanted to scream for help, but in doing so knew she may put innocent civilians in danger.

The driver stared directly at Abby and walked towards her, his focus unwavering.

"Heya. You are Abby Anderson?" he said in broken English.

Abby stared back without saying a word.

The man clicked his fingers and his two accomplices appeared with military precision. He reached into his case as Abby caught a glimpse of two more men appearing in her peripheral vision. She was now like a rabbit caught in the headlights.

"I've got for you a great surprise," said the driver, with a cock-eyed grin. "A little birdie told us where to find you!" he said, slamming the black case shut.

Abby threw her head back in fear, and before she squeezed her eyes shut, bracing herself for the worst, the last thing she saw was the sunlight glinting off the metal instrument in the man's hand.

It's been a good life, she thought. *There's things I wish I'd done...*

"This is from someone special," the assassin said, and he gave a horrible laugh. "From someone who wanted to make this day for you memorable." With the man's thick accent, he pronounced 'memorable' like *memorial.*

Goodbye, Sam...

"One-two-three!" the killer shouted. Abby put her hands to her face.

A sound rather like an agitated elephant filled the air, quickly accompanied by the rhythmic noise of guitar strings being plucked.

Abby assumed she'd been shot, and that this was the musical accompaniment to her final resting place. She opened one eye, fully expecting to be greeted by the angel Gabriel, and not by five men wearing giant sombreros with stick-on moustaches.

Her eyes took a moment to adjust to the bright sunlight, and her ears a moment longer, to the sound of Spanish guitars, trumpets, and an array of instruments which were a not-unpleasant assault on her senses.

Once her resting heart rate had returned to a level considered safe, she allowed a smile to escape her lips. The arrival of a full mariachi band on Peel Promenade was not an everyday occurrence and drew not only quite a crowd, but also an impressive shade of red from Abby's cheeks.

Abby tried to retreat into the office doorway, but the driver and lead musician were having none of it. They were relentless in their pursuit. Abby was taken by the hand and gently, but firmly, led into the middle of the road — stopping the traffic in both directions — as the rest of the band joined him, circling around her and strumming and tooting away merrily.

Ordinarily, drivers would be giving angry gestures and sounding their horns, but on this beautiful evening in Peel, the drivers climbed out of their cars and joined into the carnival atmosphere. Children abandoned their sandcastles and ran — with parents in tow — to see where the magical sound was coming from. The lead musician took Abby in his arms and danced with her to further enhance her discomfort, but, to be fair, she was now starting to embrace the craziness — even going so far as to remove her shoes so she could dance to the music.

"This is absolutely mad," she said through laughter that now flowed freely.

The music came to an end, prompting the lead musician to spin her till she was dizzy. He placed his trumpet carefully down, raised his hands above his head, and clapped as he pranced toward her. Pulled from somewhere, like a magician, a vibrant red rose appeared — tucked between his clenched teeth. He knelt in front of Abby and presented the floral tribute to her as a flurry of camera phones flashed.

She shook her head in disbelief, gratefully retrieving the flower and placing a hand over her mouth to cover her shock. The rose-bearer leapt to his feet once more, and he instructed his procession to retreat and clear the way in order to allow the street traffic to move once again. Cars eased along, returning to speed, beeping their horns in appreciation as they did so, as Abby climbed back in her shoes.

"*What* on earth is going on?" she asked, but there was no direct response. Instead, now the road was clear, the leader of the group clapped his hands once more and pointed further up the promenade.

Abby squinted, as she didn't quite trust her eyes. Her mouth dropped as a magnificent white horse pulling an equally magnificent white carriage made its way up the promenade at an elegant pace. She didn't know quite what to do as it pulled alongside. The driver of the carriage gave her a courteous nod, as the mariachi band opened the door for her and then played a further melody to see the carriage off and along on its way.

Abby slumped into the sumptuous leather seat, and, with the momentum of the horse moving forward, the coachman was in danger of seeing more than he bargained for. He kept one eye on the road ahead and with his spare hand leaned back, handing Abby a white envelope. She opened it with a broad smile across her face, before pulling out a card with exceptionally neat handwriting.

> I trust the music and carriage have set the mood
>
> To a castle for my princess where we shall have some food
>
> You'll be radiant and elegant, but you really can't be late
>
> For every minute is precious on our very first, long-awaited, date.
>
> Sam x

Abby pinched her bottom lip between her thumb and forefinger. She was desperate to keep the tears at bay for fear of wearing her mascara like Alice Cooper.

"Stupid bugger," she said softly. "Stupid, silly, daft bugger."

The castle was in spitting distance, but, fortunately for Abby, who was enjoying the journey immensely, they had to go a long way for a shortcut as direct access was a bridge across the harbour. The bridge designers had, with little foresight, apparently, not factored in enough width to accommodate a horse and cart. So the carriage had a gentle trot around Peel Harbour, giving those enjoying the sunshine from their moored boats an unexpected spectacle.

By the time the carriage pulled up at the entrance to Peel Castle, Abby's teeth had dried out from smiling so much. Peel Castle afforded a magnificent backdrop to the seaside town of Peel.

"M'lady," said the coachman, graciously offering a hand to help her down, whilst averting his gaze to spare any breach of modesty.

"Thank you," said Abby, unsure what to and where she should be going from there.

"This way, if you please," said the coachman, and he offered his arm to Abby and escorted her up the steps to the entrance of the castle. Built by Vikings in the eleventh century, it had played a pivotal role in the evolution of the isle. And, today, it would play host to Sam and Abby.

The coachman made his excuses, and he left Abby stood in the middle of an inner grass courtyard. The perimeter wall protected a number of ancient structures and Abby spun on the spot, unsure where to head. One thing she was sure about was that high heels didn't like grass. She staggered for a moment before removing her shoes, holding them in her hands. She admired the red sandstone walls and was instantly transported back to being a girl, surrounded by friends on a school outing.

Her moment of nostalgia gave way to the sound of music. She moved her head to triangulate where the sound emanated. She walked forward, and caught a glimpse of shimmering flames coming from the remnants of the castle cathedral.

Inside, two rows of candles flickered on the gentle breeze, forming a flaming path to a large wooden table

— a table which Sam, wearing an immaculate black tuxedo, stood behind. Abby was making a habit of this today, but once again gripped her bottom lip to hold back the tears. She shook her head in awe as she walked through the exquisite surroundings.

"Welcome," said Sam. He adjusted his jacket and moved out from the cover of the table towards his beautiful date for the evening.

As soon as the entirety of him was in view, Abby burst into a fit of hysterics.

"Oh my god," said Abby, snorting with laughter. "You are an absolute tool."

Sam held his hands out like a scarecrow. "What?" he said, protesting his innocence. "Don't you like the suit?"

"I like the suit," said Abby. "But I really don't think those shorts go with it. I thought you threw them away?"

"I did," said Sam. "But they must have been in a two-pack, because I found these blue ones. And, as you can see, they're as neat at the others."

"Neat?" laughed Abby. "I think you mean painted-on. They're almost indecent."

From the waist up Sam was immaculate, like a young James Bond. But, waist down, it was not so good. He'd tucked his shirt into his shorts, and he had his socks pulled up to just below his kneecaps.

"You're mad as a hatter," said Abby. "Please tell me you have alcohol?"

Sam nodded. "You'd be amazed at how many women have said that to me over the years."

"I wouldn't," replied Abby, taking a glass of something fizzy from Sam. "I really wouldn't. I'm amazed you haven't worn the wig to complete the ensemble!"

"I genuinely thought about it," he said, moving closer to her. "You look absolutely stunning, by the way," he said. "Just wow!"

Abby blushed with modesty. "What's wrong with your hand? What have you done to yourself now?" she asked, in reference to the beige bandage covering the index finger of his left hand.

"Ah, that. You'll find out. Please, take a seat," he said, pulling out a chair for Abby.

Sam clapped his hands together, and from nowhere a man in a black tuxedo appeared with violin in hand.

"Sam, you're amazing. This is stunning, truly wonderful," said Abby. "Hang on. He looks familiar. Isn't that one of the mariachi band?" she asked in reference to the man producing a haunting tune on the violin.

Sam motioned with his hand, and the violinist ripped off his moustache without missing a note. "He's a man of many talents!" he proclaimed. "Also, I'd already paid him, so thought I may as well make good use of him. So there's that," he added with a cheeky grin.

Sam disappeared from view for a moment, stepping behind a stone column. After the clattering sound of dishes threatened to disrupt the virtuoso performance, Sam returned with an enormous silver serving dish, which he placed in the centre of the table.

Sam used his fingers to act as drumsticks, and he drummed them on the tabletop to build up the anticipation. Like pulling a rabbit from a hat, he then whipped the lid off to reveal a perfectly-dressed lobster.

Abby looked at the lobster, then to Sam, and then back to the lobster. "I'm guessing the lobster did that to your finger, then?" she asked, with an expression that was a mixture of both sympathy and mirth.

"Yup. He sure did," said Sam. "This little crustaceanary cracker broke my finger. But it was worth it."

"What was?" asked Abby.

Sam bowed his head. "Delivering on a promise, Abby," he said, before taking her hand in his. He looked her in the eye as the music reverberated around the cathedral walls and the candlelight flickered on Abby's pretty face. "Abby, I said I'd catch a lobster for you, and I did. It nearly severed an artery. But I did it."

Abby leaned forward and placed the gentlest of kisses on Sam's cheek. "Thank you. Thank you for this. All of it. It's special," she said to him. "Can you do me just one favour before you sit down?"

"Of course," Sam replied.

"For the love of all that's holy, please put some trousers on. It doesn't embarrass me, mind you. It's just you've got better legs than me, and you're showing me up."

$$\mathcal{P}\,\mathsf{Q}$$

Copious amounts of wine were consumed over the course of the evening — including by the violinist, who was started to do the musical equivalent of slurring, though Sam and Abby were too preoccupied to notice. Abby couldn't have wished for a more magical location for their first date, and a more magical evening. Well, apart from the discarded shorts which hung on the side of Sam's chair, of course.

The music stopped for a moment as the violinist replenished the contents of his glass.

"What are you staring at?" asked Abby of Sam.

"You," said Sam. "I've wanted this for so long, and to be finally sat here, is, well... ace."

Abby groaned. "Ace?"

"I crumpled in the moment," replied Sam. "But, yes. Ace. Ace, brilliant, fantastic, and amazing. Thank you for being here."

Abby caressed the back of his hand. "You couldn't possibly flick those shorts from your chair, could you?" she asked. "They're quite distracting."

"I'll bet they are," Sam answered, waggling his eyebrows. He then took them and swung them playfully around his head before releasing like an elastic band.

"Thank you! Oh, something to tell you as well," she said with a hint of mystery. She held her tongue for an age.

"Well?" prompted Sam.

"I got a call today," said Abby. "From Henry."

"Who's Henry? A new client?"

"No," said Abby. "Remember Emma said his name in the lighthouse? Like she knew him?"

"No. If you'll remember, I thought I'd been mortally wounded at that point," said Sam. "But go on."

"A splinter," said Abby. "It was a splinter."

"A chunk of glass. A huge chunk," he countered.

"Anyway," she continued. "One of the police, or whatever they were, was Henry. Turns out that Henry was undercover the whole time. He'd been working with the real FBI, and was with MI6 or some James Bond-style agency. He'd worked with Emma, as it turns out, who'd had no idea throughout, of course, who he was. He had to get close to her to bring down Mr Esposito and the gang."

"Cheese and crackers!" said Sam, eloquently.

"I know! He phoned me to let me know that Emma and Madeline were safe. They're in protective custody for the time being. At least until the court case."

"That's good of him to phone you."

"I know. Emma asked him to say thank you to both of us. And she said she would pay us a visit, if she could. Oh, and the great news is that Joey is going to be fine!"

Sam smiled. He knew Abby was fond of the big guy, regardless of the fact that Joey was at one point going to be the last face she'd ever see. "Is he going to jail, then?"

"No, I think he's going to be giving evidence. Joey loved animals, and Emma's sister Madeline is a vet. So she's going to be giving him a job, as it happens."

"Bloody long phone call?" said Sam.

Abby rolled her eyes. "I'm just glad they're all okay," she said. "I'm really pleased they're okay."

Sam handed a rolled-up scroll to Abby.

"What's this?" she asked.

"Open it and you'll find out."

She used her fingernail to break a small wax seal and then unravelled a superbly illustrated certificate.

"You wanted a place on our website for all the cases we've solved," Sam explained. "But I thought we should also have a space on our office wall where we could hang a visual reminder of our work. This is the first one. You know, with a clever Sherlock Holmes styling."

Abby raised one eyebrow. "Sam, that's a wonderful idea," she said. She held the certificate out with both hands, and with the gentle illumination of the candle read the words aloud:

The Eyes Peeled Seaside Detective Agency: The Art of Forgery

"I love it," said Abby. "I think we're going to have a lot more certificates on the wall judging by how often the phone has been ringing. The old man is going to be delighted by the amount of money we're bringing in."

Sam raised his glass. "To us! To Sam and Abby and Eyes Peeled, the greatest seaside detective agency!"

Abby raised her glass. "Sam," she said calmly. "Sam, your shorts have caught on the candlestick. They're on fire."

The End

Other Books by J C Williams

If you've enjoyed this book, the author would be very grateful if you would be so kind as to leave feedback on Amazon. You can subscribe for author updates and news on new releases at:

www.authorjcwilliams.com

J C Williams
Author

authorjcwilliams@gmail.com
@jcwilliamsbooks
@jcwilliamsauthor

And if you've enjoyed this book, make sure to check out my other books as well, starting with Book Two in *The Seaside Detective Agency* series!

More...

The *Frank 'n' Stan's Bucket List* series:

The Lonely Heart Attack Club series:

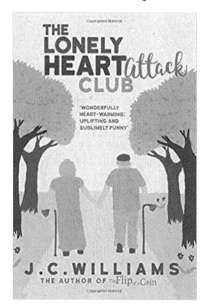

The Flip of a Coin:

And *The Bookshop by the Beach!*

And you may also wish to have a gander at my other books aimed at a younger audience...

Cabbage von Dagel   *Hamish McScabbard*

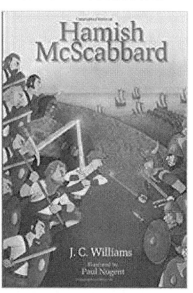

Luke 'n' Conor's Hundred-to-One Club

Deputy Gabe Rashford: Showdown at Buzzards Creek

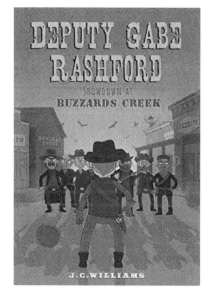

All jolly good fun!

Manufactured by Amazon.ca
Bolton, ON